SPECIAL MESSAGE TO READERS

THE ULVERSCROFT FOUNDATION
(registered UK charity number 264873)

was established in 1972 to provide funds for
research, diagnosis and treatment of eye diseases.
Examples of major projects funded by
the Ulverscroft Foundation are:-

- The Children's Eye Unit at Moorfields Eye Hospital, London
- The Ulverscroft Children's Eye Unit at Great Ormond Street Hospital for Sick Children
- Funding research into eye diseases and treatment at the Department of Ophthalmology, University of Leicester
- The Ulverscroft Vision Research Group, Institute of Child Health
- Twin operating theatres at the Western Ophthalmic Hospital, London
- The Chair of Ophthalmology at the Royal Australian College of Ophthalmologists

You can help further the work of the Foundation
by making a donation or leaving a legacy.
Every contribution is gratefully received. If you
would like to help support the Foundation or
require further information, please contact:

THE ULVERSCROFT FOUNDATION
The Green, Bradgate Road, Anstey
Leicester LE7 7FU, England
Tel: (0116) 236 4325
website: www.foundation.ulverscroft.com

MALICE IN WONDERLAND

Three tales of mystery and the macabre. When the body of a woman clothed in the scantiest of swimsuits is found lying close to the surf on the private beach of a motel, Florida Police Chief Bill Duggan faces a baffling problem. Did she accidentally drown, or commit suicide? Or has she been murdered by one of the very strange guests at the motel? In other stories, a small girl's talent in witchcraft unmasks a killer, and a man's fourth marriage has a fatal ending.

RUFUS KING

◆

MALICE IN WONDERLAND
& Other Stories

Complete and Unabridged

LINFORD
Leicester

First published in Great Britain

First Linford Edition
published 2016

*A catalogue record for this book is available
from the British Library.*

ISBN 978–1–4448–3058–3

Published by
F. A. Thorpe (Publishing)
Anstey, Leicestershire

Set by Words & Graphics Ltd.
Anstey, Leicestershire
Printed and bound in Great Britain by
T. J. International Ltd., Padstow, Cornwall

This book is printed on acid-free paper

Contents

Let Her Kill Herself

The motel, hugging the shore of the lazy sea, was called Black's. Located on the Gold Coast between Miami Beach and Fort Lauderdale, it offered in its single-storied fashion luxurious living at a good stiff price. There were the customary swimming pool, a private beach, a cocktail room that was totally atmospheric, and, if you were silly enough to patronize it, a small restaurant that served luncheon snacks.

On the beach proper, artistically conceived as a thatched job from Pago-Pago, was the combined living quarters and beach-wear shop of the lifeguard, Oscar Bjorgsen. He lived there, not with a wife as yet, but with Jimmy Hart, the night-shift bartender of the cocktail lounge. They also shared a sporty convertible, and their melting point toward dames could be reached with the glow from a match.

As Jimmy often remarked during the next six months, at which time a fresher conversation piece developed in the form of a poisoned divorcée from Akron, nothing could have been smoother than Thursday night. The regulars were all in their regular places and he noted, while stirring two manhattans for the Cardigan Bags, the last element in what he called the Dean-Spang situation coming into the lounge.

She was registered as Miss Theda Sangford, and the briefest glance stamped her as a woman of mystery, her looks being darkly exotic and her costumes as revealing as a crystal ball. Naturally she slinked, with her insurable legs and contest-winning torso lending to all her movements the liquid co-ordination of quicksilver. You were prepared for about any sort of contralto foreign accent and were consequently rocked when her voice turned out to be solid Bronx as chirped by a bird.

The bar closed at two, and just before the hour Miss Sangford said to Jimmy, 'Drop off a bottle on your way by, will you, Jimmy?'

'The usual?'

'Yes. Maybe you'd better make it two.'

'Glad to, Miss Sangford. In about half an hour?'

'That will be fine.'

Jimmy put the bar to bed, and Eric Havermay, who had the bar concession, took the night's receipts, and they drank a brew together.

'I've got a feeling,' Havermay said. 'I've got a feeling that something's coming up and I don't like it. It's a bad situation.'

'Young Dean?' Jimmy asked.

'Both him and his mother and Spang and Sangford.'

'Setups like that are a dime a dozen down here, and you know it.'

'I do, and I know what comes of them. Trouble. Who's the bottles for?'

'Sangford. She wants me to drop them on the way by.'

'She's swimming in it right now.'

'Well?'

'Well, just this. It's what I've been talking about. It's exactly when it happens. Let them put away enough of that stuff and they turn into Annie Oakleys. Not one time when it's ever happened down here have they been sober.'

Jimmy said again, 'Well?'

Havermay wrestled with a few sparse shreds of an early-New England conscience, one that had been a shining field, sumptuous with a crop of basic virtues and tailor-made niceties. But a man had to live. And he had to get it while the getting was good. For a buck you could stretch a little, because a buck was a buck.

He didn't like to do this stretching and would often say so in the didactic tones of a moralist. But he did it, nevertheless. She was a good customer. Good for twenty bucks a night.

'All right,' he said. 'Let her knock herself out. Let her kill herself if she wants to.'

Havermay left. The stock was padlocked and the lights extinguished, with the exception of one torchère on a driftwood stand near the door. Jimmy killed a palmetto bug (Florida for flying cockroach), stepping on its paper-thin armor plate and kicking it under the duckwalk.

The bar was in order, the ash trays clean and rightly spaced along its length, the glasses shiny clean, and in the shadows of the night-filled room a white hand moved.

Its pale arc hovered over near the table where young Dean always sat with his watchdog Bert Jackson, and Jenny Spang. Jimmy went over to the woman who was seated there.

'It's closing time, Miss Fernandez,' he said.

She was an attractive woman in a heavy way, dark-eyed and dark-haired and dressed on the ornamental side, with a bank of expensive bracelets on her left forearm, and with large earrings of intricate gold.

'Yes,' she said, 'I know. I am depressed. There is a mist, very black. Not for me, you understand, but for others. For that alive young man and the girl he should marry. I grope after their future, but my fingers touch nothing.'

Jimmy summed up his knowledge of Miss Fernandez. Rich, very possibly a Puerto Rican of unusually distinguished ancestry, a good but never excessive tipper, a conservative drinker, and neither a man-snatcher nor a table-hopper. Her odd way of expressing herself was a minor quirk. But this 'black-mist' business verged on the screwball. His lifeguard roommate had told him of her strong hobby for collecting shells at odd hours along the tide edge.

What Jimmy had failed to appreciate was that Miss Fernandez, apart from quirks, was an observant woman in her own strange way and to an all but mathematical degree.

'I stay here,' she went on, 'and I think. You do not mind?'

'Not a bit.'

'You are kind. Good night.'

'Good night.'

There was no moon, and the coral walk past the unit patios was silver against velvet grays, and the surface of the swimming pool was silver, and amber light diffused through the Sangford unit's Venetian blinds.

Jimmy pressed the door button and heard the soft chime and her voice in its birdlike chirp call, 'Come in.'

He entered an empty living room, and her voice called again from behind a closed door, 'Jimmy? Just leave the bottles, will you?'

'On the desk, Miss Sangford.'

He placed the bottles on the desk and then, under a swift compulsion which he could not at the moment nor at any later time understand, called, 'Miss Sangford — '

'What, Jimmy?'

'Have you been bothered by any — well, what you might call premonitions? Like, say, groping around in a mist?'

'Not me, Jimmy boy. Tonight the world is my oyster. Forget the creeps, pal, and go home and sleep it off.'

Jimmy went, a lithe shade through the stillness of the semi-tropical night, and the memory of her laughter did not reassure him, for the feeling that Havermay had felt was dominant, and the crack about mists by Miss Fernandez and the look of seeing in her eyes.

★ ★ ★

The night rolled on with the homecoming of the late ones from the clubs and supper traps. Young Ernest Dean and Jenny Spang and Ernest's watchhound Bert Jackson came back from dancing in the Coral Room of the Chalefont Towers, and a familiar look passed between Ernest and Bert. It was from habit entirely understandable by each, and a cartoonist would have symbolized it with pupils in the shape of dollar marks.

Bert Jackson's exact position in the Dean ménage was the subject of considerable conjecture among the cocktail brigade. In appearance Bert resembled a somewhat ripened Dead End Kid, with the build of a wrestler and a rarely produced infectious smile that would break through the dark glower. He wore expensive clothes and his manners were honed to an edge that would have brought a fan-flick of approval from Emily Post.

He made a fetish of cleanliness, going to indescribable lengths of care and detail about the scrubbed freshness of his person, and somewhere in the dimming past lay a background of both money and gentility.

The women's section of the regulars considered Bert's role of Little-Shepherd-to-sonny-boy as so much eyewash, even though Ernest's pockets were loaded with his mother's money, and an occasional break either at the track or in one of the sub-rosa gaming casinos further increased his freight of funds.

No, the gossipers decided that Bert's real job lay in having an affair with Mama Dean. This struck them as being completely in line, Mrs. Dean being a loaded widow and still quite able to stack up with the best of them. With her slim, well-kept figure and shoulder-length hair brushed under and tinted a pale gold, it was a commonplace for her to be mistaken for Ernest's sister, especially as his manner held a touch of grave maturity at odd variance with his actual age.

Bert sheered off into the Dean apartment, and Ernest went with Jenny into the adjoining Spang patio. They sat on a metal white-enameled settee and in the darkness under the pinpoint individuality of the stars they were very close and in each other's arms. Their voices were quiet, very low. But they were not low enough to be muted in the hush which was complete but for the slumberous break of surf along the shore. Ernest held her more tightly while the warmth of her cheek became fire against his.

11

'I guess you know why I drink,' he said. 'At the tough times, I mean. I get so drunk I don't remember the next day what I've done or what I've said. Everything is an absolute blank.'

'Bert's paid to stop you from that, isn't he?'

'Yes, and to hand in the field reports to Mother. Well, he's paid to forget about it too. By me. I tell her I've lost at the horses or dice and then I'll hand the money over to Bert for covering up for me.' He added with the acid intensity of youth, in a swelter of self-disgust that gagged him like gall, 'I'm no good. Really, Jenny, I mean it. I'm not honest with anybody. Even with you. Mother is the most wonderful woman in the world. She's done everything for me, made every sacrifice.'

With a wisdom beyond her years Jenny kept her counsel. Actually she regarded Mrs. Dean as the blood kin of those cannibal fish who devour their own young.

But she did say, 'She'll never let you get married. She'll never give you up.'

'I know, and there are times when I hate her. I've never said this to a living soul before, Jenny, but sometimes I've wished her dead.'

'You can't help that. It's the chained feeling. It's that way with me too. I go crazy at times when Mama shoves me at some rich old goat. Then her heart — '

Ernest nodded. 'I know. Mother's, too.'

One thing that Mrs. Dean and Mrs. Spang had strongly in common was their hearts. Each had a convenient 'condition' as one of the leash effects that could be brought into play at will — Mrs. Dean succumbing to dizziness followed by a faint, and Mrs. Spang being adroit at a frightening spell of last-minute gasps.

Both women kept on hand appropriate props to bolster the illusion. Mrs. Spang was never without her ampules of amyl nitrite, and Mrs. Dean had ever within her reach a vial of strychnine pills.

Ernest belted himself still further. 'I'm not even a man. But I will be, Jenny — now that I've got you. I'll clear up one mess I'm in that you don't even know about, that I never want you to know

13

about. I'm going to clear it up in the morning once and for all.'

A low whistle came from the Dean apartment, signaling that Mrs. Dean was awake.

'That's Bert.'

They hurriedly but still moltenly kissed good night, and Ernest left.

The water was warm and infinitely soothing to Miss Sangford's admirable body, in particular to her head, which was entertaining a convention of riveters. It was also entertaining a few doubts.

She felt uncertain that her course was the right one. It had been simple enough to trace him down to this motel called Black's. An item in one of the cafe-society gossip columns had taken care of that. But this anger, this decision to smash, to rip things wide simply for the balm of revenge, a revenge that would surely prove costly — was that smart?

She closed her eyes and in the comforting water was in a world alone, and with this sense of aloneness a familiar fear stole over her. The sense of solitude was suddenly gone. But the fear remained.

She screamed as the hands closed about her ankles.

The familiar hands.

The water, as the grip tightened and gave an upward yank, choked short her scream.

★   ★   ★

It was several hours later that dawn paled the east while bands of cerise roped low above the horizon of the sea, and Miss Fernandez, brilliant in a flamingo swim suit, walked down to the tide edge for a dip and to gather shells.

Actually it was an almost impossible hour for the search, as the air and sea and sand were bathed in a pale luminosity rather than true light. But it was a physical action, like fingering beads, one that kept her body occupied while her real concentration lay in her thoughts.

A movement off to her left in the Deans' corner unit of the motel caught her attention. It registered itself as the somewhat careful closing of the apartment's beach door. The door was being

15

pulled gently to from the inside.

Then almost at once, within the perimeter visible to her shell-seeking eyes, appearing beyond its circumference as she moved slowly forward, was the body of a woman. Shock confused her while the knowledge slowly registered that it was Miss Sangford and that Miss Sangford was dead.

Miss Fernandez's notion of corpse-discovery procedure in the United States was exclusively based on Spanish translations of paperbacks. From them she had gleaned the inflexible rule that never must anything be touched on the X-spot until the police arrive. Also, apart from being ignorant as to how to go about doing it, she did not consider using artificial respiration. Having passed through numerous Puerto Rican political revolutions, she considered herself expert at recognizing the permanently dead when she saw them.

Speed in informing the proper authorities was of high importance. She fished a coin purse from her bag of shells and, going to a telephone booth attached to the lifeguard's shop, dialed the operator and asked to be connected with the police.

'An emergency?' the operator asked.

'Very. A woman. She has been drowned.'

'I will connect you directly with Chief Duggan's home. The men at the station will be out on patrol.'

Bill Duggan, in his thirties, was steeped in the leisureliness of Florida living, but in spite of a retarded outlook on the illegal antics of his fellow men he was thoroughly up to date on most new phases of criminology. The drowned were no novelty for him. Before joining the force he had been a lifeguard, and his knowledge of crazy bathers, sane fish, and wholesome, sticky, tangy salt water was encyclopedic.

When he reached Black's private beach, accompanied by the handsome hulk of Officer Alan Day, he found Miss Fernandez standing in guardian vigil beside the body.

She said, well composed, 'One thought at first, for the briefest moment, that she slept. But no. As the gentlemen can observe, she is dead.'

Duggan observed. The body, clothed in the scantiest of swim suits, lay on one side close to the surf. There was no bathing cap, and strands of hair partially masked a profile which by its tautness suggested that rigidity had begun. Duggan knelt and confirmed that rigor mortis already was attacking the face and jaw.

'Will I get to work?' Day asked.

Duggan shook his head. 'No use, Al. It's too late. Call up and cancel the pulmotor and tell Roth we'll want pictures. Also, ask Tropical to send an ambulance.'

Duggan studied the sand patterns dried on the flesh. He brushed back the clinging hair the better to see the features. His fingers paused, then cautiously explored the scalp. There was a degree of dampness at the hair base which the high humidity of the atmosphere had kept from drying out, even though, to judge from the onset of rigor, death had occurred at least two hours previously.

He leaned quite closely to the hair and sniffed. He found some bruise marks around the ankles which interested him. He took a notebook from his pocket and turned back to Miss Fernandez.

'May I have your full name, please?'

'Loreta Janeta Fernandez.'

'You are a guest here, Miss Fernandez?'

'For one week and for one week more. Then I am home again in San Juan.'

'Do you know who this is?'

'She too is a guest. A Miss Theda Sangford, from the City of New York. Beyond that I am ignorant but for an incident of uncertain value. I hesitate to speak up. He is a good, a nice young man but badly controlled by his mother. You have the expression — a mama's boy?'

'Yes.'

'It would be distasteful to me to believe he would permit this poor one to drown. You understand?'

'Perfectly.' Duggan smiled faintly. 'Who is he, and why do you think he may have?'

'He is Ernest Dean. He is a youth very stalwart in the extreme but with blood that turns from red to milk beneath his mother's touch.' Miss Fernandez pointed, emphasizing the gesture with a deepening intensity of expression. 'I behold the movement of that door. It is being pulled shut from within. This will be but a minute ago, at the hour when nobody is abroad. You will weigh the event of this door judicially? With compassion? You will consider his youth and that in all virtue he may have tried to save her? In vain. And then in panic, upon observing my approach, he fled.'

It was curious, Duggan thought, how patly a layman could tie up a homicide and present its solution with an absurd assurance to a trained observer.

'Evidently you know of some connection between this woman and Mr. Dean,' he said.

Miss Fernandez looked somberly wise. She struggled to capsule within a few words a panorama of a situation that had, for a considerable time now, been disturbing her inwardly.

'It is deeper than the shopworn convention one calls the eternal triangle. Its roots lie in the character of that dangerous woman.'

'This woman? Miss Sangford?'

She expressed a shrug of impatience at his ineptitude in failing to grasp instantly the implacable chains that fettered young Dean.

'No, the roots lie in his mother. She is

rich, but fantastically rich. Her jewels alone are worth a fortune. She has put the world at his feet, but he dare not explore it without her visa.'

'What I suppose you're getting at, Miss Fernandez, is that Miss Sangford made a serious attempt to snag the boy.'

'What else? Not alone I, but all the guests knew it to be true. I was in the cocktail room on the evening when this greedy one arrived. How shall I tell you?'

She looked at him and beyond him and back to the scene of Theda Sangford's initial entrance one week earlier into the cocktail lounge, adjusting the main characters (young Dean and Bert) into their proper place on stage, which was a table beneath a mounted marlin on the west wall.

She pictured herself seated near enough to this table for observation but quite beyond earshot of what was being said. Then she brought the body of Theda Sangford from its stiffening posture on the sand into an effect of life that was convincing in spite of her outlandish way of expressing herself.

'One watched her entrance, which was in the manner where every step is a provocation. One watched her pause and survey the field. One watched her remove a cigarette from a jeweled case and seat herself on a banquette adjoining the table of Mr. Dean. It was a display of virtuosity which would have brought an acclaim to a Cleopatra. Almost immediately she asked him for a light. Ah — the impact!'

'On Dean?'

'I shall tell you this. You may regard it as having been equivalent to the effect upon a man which would be produced only by a cobra with business in its eye.'

'Well, after all,' Duggan said equably, 'if there was that initial aversion to her on his part — I'm afraid I just don't understand.' She said with courteous impatience that he did not understand his own sex, nor did he evidently comprehend the power of sex in itself, particularly when it was wielded by an accomplished woman. This, of course, was absolute slander, but Duggan let it pass.

'You will accept that by last night she had him in her power.' Miss Fernandez launched into the full-bodied stream of her narrative. 'You will regard me at the hour of cocktails, seated at a vantage point from which one aspect of this tragedy could be observed very clearly.'

'Just let me get this straight. You are now talking about last night?'

'I am. To my right, at their accustomed table beneath that stiff, stuffed fish are seated Mr. Dean and the leechlike Mr. Jackson.'

'Why leechlike?'

'He is an agent engaged by Mrs. Dean to report every movement of her son. So they sit there and they solace themselves with double daiquiris while awaiting the arrival of Miss Spang.'

'Double daiquiris. How was young Dean? Would you say that he was drunk?'

'He had taken too much to drink. But it is not Miss Spang who accepts the waiting chair. It is this poor one, here.' Miss Fernandez lowered a glance of Christian commiseration on the dead. 'I must tell you that Mr. Jackson is temporarily away, gone through that door on which is the silhouette of a running man.

'For an instant I am bemused by Francine, the barmaid, who is producing at my table a rum punch. When again I study Mr. Dean it is to see that his face is as white as the under portion of that terrible fish. He is saying, forgetting his true gentility, 'Shut up!' And this unfortunate one employs upon her lips a smile of pure evil and remarks, 'By daybreak, understand? Be there or you will be a very, very sorry little boy.'' Miss Fernandez concluded simply, 'She stands. She goes. It is the curtain of her scene.'

It also, Duggan realized, planted Dean squarely on the spot.

'You said one aspect, Miss Fernandez. Were there others?'

The sun rose leisurely above the ocean's rim. The sands were fired with gold, and only the flesh of Miss Sangford retained a mortal pallor. The tide on ebb sighed backward into the sea, and Miss Fernandez emerged with another small bouquet from the garden of her thoughts.

'After dinner, at the hour when the television is in force, seated on the ban-quette next to mine are Mrs. Dean and

Mrs. Spang. Ah, that one!'

Duggan asked with reasonable uncertainty, 'Which?'

'Mrs. Spang, the mother of that charming, fragrant girl. A woman, you must grasp, of ice, with a cold prettiness that is beginning to melt with age. As one woman has put it to me, she is a Custer in Schiaparelli embarked on her ultimate stand.'

'Busted?'

'So it is said. It is either a marriage of importance for her daughter, or the end. The Dean fortune exposes itself as her last gun.'

'Well, from what you've told me he seems willing enough. Or was Miss Sangford a serious threat?'

'You will consider the conversation which I overheard when the scenario on the television screen concerns itself with pantomime. You will listen, please, to Mrs. Dean: 'If Ernest were to marry and leave me I would cut his allowance off completely.' To this decision Mrs. Spang replies: 'I suppose you know best, dear. But that woman is determined. Why don't you go to Nassau until she leaves?' And now, the crux. It is the voice of Mrs. Dean: 'I shall meet this danger in my own manner — and never by running away.''

Miss Fernandez reached the end of her disclosures and obviously waited for Duggan to take up the ball. What she expected, he imagined, was a swift descent on his part upon young Dean, who, being a fine, upstanding American youth (no matter how badly mother-ridden), would obligingly admit that he had met Miss Sangford by appointment at daybreak. Under the harmless cloak of taking an early-morning dip, of course. It would then be revealed that the dip had backfired and that young Dean, callowly panic-stricken, had taken off for home base.

★ ★ ★

Duggan was saved from disillusioning Miss Fernandez as to the number of holes in this amateurs slice of Swiss by a group strolling toward them from the motel. It was led by Officer Day.

Duggan explained to Roth, a police technician, what pictures to take, specifying in particular close-ups of the ankles and the hair and the patterns left on the dead woman's flesh by the dried sand. He suggested that they first be outlined, say with a lipstick.

He wanted a complete set of Miss Sangford's fingerprints transmitted telephotographically to New York and Washington, after which the boys could remove the body to the morgue space of Tropical to be held for the medical examiner.

He left a final suggestion that a detailed search be made of the shoreline to the north and south. If the ocean had been kind enough to disgorge it, he would like the bathing cap that was missing from Miss Sangford's head. Presumably it had been lost during the usual convulsive struggles that precede a death by drowning. Then he went to the manager's office and called up Sibley.

Dr. Frank Sibley, pathologist at Tropical General Hospital, was the appointed associate medical examiner for South Broward County. He was young, he was a perfectionist, and he was adroit. Homicide held for him the peculiar fascination of a Chinese puzzle, one of the ring sort that requires the most delicate patience to solve.

Duggan explained.

He said to Sibley in conclusion, 'One thing I wish you'd do at once, Frank. Subject the heart to the Gettler test.'

Sibley was impressed.

'So it's one of those?'

'I think it is. Let me know, will you, as soon as you've checked? As early this afternoon as possible?'

'Look, Bill, the solutions for that test have to stand overnight. There will be nothing on it decisive before tomorrow morning.'

Waldo Barcombe, the motel manager, came into the room from his quarters and looked frowzily at Duggan. Waldo's job was largely titular, as his wife Kitty did the managing and the actual work of keeping the place running smoothly. In spite of his post before the public, Waldo was not in reality an affable man, being given to blanket dislikes, such as a loathing of all

Southerners, all jobs where the slightest physical exertion was required, and any lack of tastiness in the preparation by Kitty of his meals. He was an all-round coddled egg.

'Hello, Bill,' he said. 'Kitty's told me. There's always one like that Miss Sangford. A troublemaker.'

'Tell me about her.'

'What do we know about any of them? What they tell us, that's all. She had the dough and she laid it on the line.'

'For how long?'

'Two weeks.'

'What else?'

'A New York address in the East Fifties.'

'How about mail since she's been here?'

'No mail.'

'Phone calls?'

Waldo picked up the telephone and said to the girl on the front-office switchboard, 'About Miss Sangford, Mabel — '

'Isn't it terrible!'

'No, it isn't. She probably took a swim while potted and got what was coming to her.'

'Oh, Mr. Barcombe! The Bible says — '

'Never mind what the Bible says. Tell me if she received any telephone calls while she's been here.'

'Not while I was on.'

'Check with Pete about nights.'

'I have. That is, he mentioned it to me only this morning when I took over. Not a call, and what with her figure he thought it peculiar.'

Waldo hung up and relayed all this to Duggan.

'What made you say she had it coming to her?' Duggan asked.

'Latching onto young Dean for one thing. Trying to take him away from Jenny Spang. Boy, has that guy's mama got dough. She's even got a watchdog-bodyguard to ride herd on him, she keeps him so loaded. No kidding.'

'Bert Jackson? Is that his name?'

'You know about it?'

'A Miss Fernandez briefed me.'

'That bird. She flops around in fogs feeling for things. I think she's half cracked.'

'Possibly. Let me in Miss Sangford's apartment, will you, Waldo?'

Waldo took a passkey from the desk drawer.

'Let's go.'

While Duggan searched the Sangford unit with the zealot nicety of a Carrie Nation sniffing out a dram, the sun rose higher into the warmth of morning, while the motel stirred to life and to the impact of snowballing rumors.

Among the feminine division these embraced such positively known facts as that that vampire had accidentally drowned — she had committed suicide — she had been dragged beneath the waves by (a) Mrs. Dean, (b) Mrs. Spang, (c) Jenny Spang, (d) Ernest. She had fought madly for her life and had been bruised all over, several people knowing several people who had heard her perfectly ghastly dying shrieks (sea gulls). She had succumbed without a struggle while in a disgraceful drunken stupor — with the only point of complete agreement among the ladies being that Officer Day was a doll.

The local press — Fort Lauderdale, Hollywood, Miami — was as yet cold to the story, and the incident was tactfully dropped into the category of a sadly drowned tourist. As such it was quietly underplayed, with the virtuous hope being advanced that amateur swimming visitors to our golden strands would take proper heed and quit venturing into our gentle, delightful, azure-blue sea before the efficient life-guards came on duty and would be on hand to fish them out of it again.

Duggan ended his inch-by-inch search and had Roth take such photographs as he felt the county prosecutor could use in evidence. These included three sets of finger-prints on one of the two bottles of scotch that Jimmy had left. Duggan wanted them put through the mill.

Then he said to Waldo, 'I'm about ready for young Dean.'

Waldo looked at him with the pleading eyes of an unfed seal.

'Take it easy with the kid, will you, Bill? They're paying top seasonal rental, and what's more she's got enough of the stuff to slam the pick of the legal hot shots in your face if you step out of line.'

He would not, Duggan promised, step out of line, and they walked to the Dean apartment, and Waldo pressed the button for the door chime. Sun smashed purple flame into the bougainvillea in one corner of the patio, and only the surf on the shore made any sound, and the chime died into this silence. Then the door opened, and Duggan had his first view of Mrs. Dean.

Even though the hour was only half-past eight she presented a picture of competent preservation. Her gold hair shone from its brushing and the expensive sheen from an imported brilliantine. Her face was in order, and a deceptively simple cotton dress suggested the freshness of jonquils on a sunny hill.

Waldo smiled managerially.

'You've heard, I suppose,' he said.

'Yes, I've heard.'

'These lamentable, these stupid accidents!'

She played docilely along in her soft, rich voice, flickering her long-lashed glance at Duggan.

'Always so tragic,' she agreed. 'Especially with the middle-aged.'

'Middle — ! Miss Sangford?'

'Oh, easily, I should think, a contemporary of my own. Won't you come in?'

'Thank you, I can't. I've the usual thousand things to do and now with this on top of it. I just wanted to introduce Bill Duggan, our chief of police. Then I'll run along.'

Mrs. Dean extended a firm, cold hand. 'Chief Duggan?'

'Mrs. Dean.'

They shook hands, and Waldo ran along to attend to his thousand things, which were nothing more arduous than a head dive back onto a foam-rubber mattress. Duggan followed Mrs. Dean into the living room, where she asked him to sit down and then arranged herself in a formal posture on a lounge. She sat there, very composed, and observed him with a polite attention.

'I would like to talk with your son, Mrs. Dean.'

'Ernest is asleep, Mr. Duggan. Drugged, really. He suffered a rather shocking experience this morning. Around daybreak to be exact. It came as a climax to a heavy night, and the combination jolted his nerves severely. I insisted on his taking two of my pills. Luminal.'

Duggan smiled back at her understandingly. A good deal more understandingly than she knew. He admired her technique in launching the attack against himself, the enemy.

'The shocking experience. You refer to his appointment with Miss Sangford?'

Mrs. Dean gazed at him steadily with eyes that were not quite violet, not quite green, and the social set of her smile remained unaltered.

'Of course you would know about that. I believe one of the barmaids — Francine — spread the word? Or anyone else having cocktails within earshot of Miss Sangford's voice. Have you ever noted the muted quality of some bars, especially those that go in for Liberace lighting like the one here?'

'Yes, I have. An added decibel of sound in a person's voice — '

'Exactly. As for the rendezvous, it never took place. Miss Sangford was lying on the sand, drowned, when Ernest went down to the shore. As I have said, the shock of it, added to a terrific hangover — '

'I can well imagine.' He added sympathetically, 'It must have been pretty tough to make him fail to notify either the management or the police.'

She looked back at him calmly and permitted him to light the cigarette she had taken from a box on the coffee table between them.

'Obviously that would occur to you, Mr. Duggan. It would occur to anybody. I was awake when Ernest returned. I heard him being violently ill by the beach door. You may have noticed that its upper half is glassed? I went to him and could see the beach through the windowpanes. I saw that Puerto Rican woman, Miss Fernandez. I saw Miss Fernandez find Miss Sangford's body and then saw her go to the telephone booth at the lifeguard's shop. The call was to the police, to you, wasn't it, Mr. Duggan?'

'Yes.'

'I felt confident that it would have been and gave my full attention to Ernest. Bert helped me. Bert Jackson, my son's friend. After we had put Ernest to bed I looked out again on the beach, and you and that other officer had taken over.'

Duggan let the explanation rest in a quiet that grew prolonged to a limit where the smile was gone from Mrs. Dean's carnation-painted lips.

She began to feel it intolerable and said, 'Well, Mr. Duggan?'

'Did you also hear your son when he left for the beach, Mrs. Dean?'

'I am a very light sleeper, and there is little that I do not hear at night. Ernest got up and went out not more than a quarter of an hour before I heard him return. In the condition that I've told you.' Her expression grew more strained. 'Is it the reason for the rendezvous that is puzzling you?'

'In a way.'

'Now really, Mr. Duggan, with a woman of her type, why should it? My son is a perfectly normal young man.'

'It is the secrecy that has me bothered.'

'Nonsense. Were you never, at Ernest's age, shall we say, similarly involved?'

'No, neither then nor now. You see, I am still a bachelor, Mrs. Dean.'

It took a full moment for the

implication to sink in, and the effect of it on Mrs. Dean was appalling.

'Bachelor — bachelor?'

'Surely you knew that Miss Sangford was your son's wife?'

Her words were spaced like the death roll of a heart slowing down.

'I do not believe you, Mr. Duggan.'

He took a paper from a jacket pocket and handed it to her. 'The marriage certificate,' he said. 'She had hidden it rather cleverly among facial tissues. Evidently Miss Sangford was afraid it would be searched for.'

He did not, Mrs. Dean noticed, directly specify that the search would have been made by Ernest, although he obviously seemed to imply it. Her eyes lingered in total disbelief on the certificate's date, which was two months ago, and on the place, which was the Borough of Manhattan.

'I did not know,' she said with difficulty. She managed to stand up, to fight the conflicting waves of nausea and rage that swept through her. 'Would — would you be so kind as to leave me, Mr. Duggan? I find it impossible to concentrate.'

'Perhaps after an hour or two, Mrs. Dean?'

'Thank you. Surely then, yes.'

'If you will let me have the marriage certificate, please?'

'This? Oh yes.' The habit of power, the years of domination which, since her husband's death, she had enjoyed upon her solid, unassailable pedestal of a woman of social standing and of great wealth — all of those assets were returning in freshening trickles, and she said in her normal manner, 'Why do you want it?'

Duggan placed the certificate in his pocket. 'Possible evidence, Mrs. Dean.'

'Of what?'

'Motive.'

'I may seem stupid, but motive for what?'

'The murder of your son's wife, Mrs. Dean.'

★ ★ ★

The hour was ten-thirty of that Friday morning when Dr. Sibley, fully breakfasted and accompanied by a stenographer, entered the morgue in the new wing of Tropical General. They observed, resting on a broad table equipped with running water and adequate drainage, its surface brilliant under a flood of fluorescent lighting, the unclothed body of Miss Sangford.

From glassed-in cabinets along the wall Sibley selected, in addition to the usual tools, a couple of Erlenmeyer flasks. He prepared a silver nitrate solution, a potassium iodide solution, and a starch citrate mixture. He took delicate precautions that water should not contaminate the blood, wiping dry the surface of the heart and the knife, and making certain that the pipette and the receiving flasks were dry.

He did such things as had to be done and then set the solutions to one side. He looked at his watch. Possibly toward tomorrow morning he could let Duggan know the result.

By noon he had completed such other tests and observations as the regular autopsy procedure made mandatory. Two facts he was prepared to let Duggan definitely know: Miss Sangford had been pregnant and

Miss Sangford had been drunk.

Duggan digested this preliminary report of Sibley's during a luncheon of broiled snook in the company of Officer Day.

'It's wrapped up,' Day said. 'The rest is mere routine.'

Duggan deposited a fish bone on his plate and helped himself to some more coleslaw.

'You sound like Miss Fernandez,' he said.

'I do? Well, what do you know!'

'Until the Gettler test comes through we're sticking our necks out a mile if we so much as point a finger at him.'

'I don't get it. Take the setup. Money-bags Mama ready to cut his allowance if he steps out of line, and for him, in her book, wedding bells spell for whom the bell tolls — boy, am I good.'

'About as good as last week's herring.'

'Nuts, Chief. What happens? He gets potted a couple of months back and wakes up married to Little Egypt and starts paying her off to keep her from telling Mama. And I suggest that Bloodhound Jackson is the go-between.'

'That much I will grant you.'

'Chief, a child could figure this with his little hands tied behind his back. Seriously, Mama carts him down here to chill to death for the winter and he runs into the Spang number and he's gone. Real gone.'

'Okay. And he's also a married man.'

'What's so funny about that?'

'I wouldn't know.'

'So Sangford trails him. Why? Because she comes into her wits on one fine morning and finds out that she is in a delicate condition.'

'Brother, are you slicing it nice.'

'All right, so I was brought up refined. Well, she knows the score and she figures the angles this way and she figures them that. If Mama finds out her apple pie is married he is out on his neck and headed for Skid Row. But. I say but.'

'Sure, sure, and the ace in the hole is a darling grandchild, who, to ape your refined language, is two months en route on the Storkville trolley, and the fact makes Mama Dean starry-eyed with joy and her flinty heart just melts. Al, you've not only read a book, you've been glued to TV.'

'Cut it, Chief. Now what does Sangford find when she lands here? She finds her legally wedded husband overboard about the Spang twist. So she takes second choice and says to Dean, 'You will pay me off and pay through the nose. I will then quietly divorce you or get an annulment, whichever you like.' The kid says he'll pay, and she fixes it for the pay-off to be down at the beach this morning at daybreak.'

'Why? Why daybreak?'

'Can I read the minds of a couple of mixed-up kids?'

'If Sangford was a kid, bud, I'm a baby movie star.'

'All right, so she's got a few miles on her. They close the deal and go for a swim to make the meeting look good, and lover boy sees it's a golden opportunity for yanking her under — with all his troubles, big and little, gone forever. I'm telling you that Oswald Pinker, our slap-happy county prosecutor, will love it. He'll be delirious.'

'He'll be psychotic if we give him the case as it now stands. It's still as phony as a hustler's smile.'

★ ★ ★

Miss Fernandez drew reflectively toward the end of her luncheon. She was a hearty eater and a deliberate one, with very few epicurean tastes, and the food of the motel's restaurant did not desolate her appetite. There was an air of peculiar waiting. The room was unusually full, and it occurred to her that death and the police had fused the variegated guests into a group that instinctively herded together and set itself apart as a unit, as being something special.

The focal point of the diners, naturally, was the table at which Mrs. Dean sat with her son and Bert Jackson. Miss Fernandez cordially approved of Mrs. Dean's decision upon this public appearance, terming it in a sense the bravado of position — of Mrs. Dean's position in the social world — and this carrying of her rarefied environment like a shield of glass around her.

Of secondary interest were the Spangs. Both mother and daughter offered that setness of expression which renders the otherwise superb waxwork figures of Madame Tussaud's just short of being lifelike. They accomplished the physical acts of eating and speaking while giving the impossible effect of being in a state of arrested motion.

Mrs. Spang displayed her mildewing prettiness in full exhibition style, but it was no go. Nor was the virginal loveliness of Jenny any more than a flower-frail veiling for the deathblow to her love caused by the knowledge that Ernest had been married when . . .

Miss Fernandez smiled.

The knowledge that Ernest Dean and Theda Sangford had been man and wife had passed the rumor stage and was an accepted fact. There was a fascination, even a charm, about murder, and a hundredfold more so when the protagonists were right under your eyes.

Any notion of accidental drowning had been thrown out of the window. And over all (it was like viewing an artist on the high trapeze who at any moment might miss and plummet to death) was the chilling cliché that 'murder breeds.' That it breeds if and as necessity dictates. Until the hand of the killer is stilled.

The seeming inactivity of the police and of the county prosecutor's office and what appeared to be a dawdling and blasé attitude were considered curious. By Miss Fernandez most of all. She considered it not only curious but dangerous.

Such were the red wraiths in her mist. They were tentatively identified, but not with enough clear assurance as yet to permit her to issue solemn warnings. For her to say: You must guard yourself by light of heaven and in dark of night when the variety of death is legion. You must even look beneath the mask of love.

Would she be believed? Miss Fernandez sighed deeply over a forkful of lime pie. She would be heeded no more than people had heeded the warnings of Cassandra or any of the ancient seeresses when their prophecies were not a rosy pink.

One gesture, however, she did manage to make when, upon leaving the dining room, she found herself alongside Jenny Spang. Briefly she pressed the girl's hand and murmured, 'Courage, little one! Take heart!'

★   ★   ★

By three o'clock the wind had freshened in the south, rolling up moderate combers to fracture in spumy sheets along the beach and driving determined nature boys behind the shelter of canvas windbreaks. Small-craft warnings were up from Palm Beach down through the Keys.

Duggan, as he approached the Dean patio, noted Ernest and his personal St. Bernard, Bert Jackson, giving a studied impersonation of indolence on a couple of steamer chairs. Both stood as he walked in and both, in their trunks, were like copper-coated specimens of the 'after' photographs in a physical culture magazine. Of the two, in the matter of chest mattresses, Bert had the edge on Ernest by a fistful of hair.

Duggan said he was Chief Duggan, and Ernest said yes, he knew. Then they all shook hands and sat.

'I guess Mother gave you a pretty good line-up on what happened,' Ernest said.

'Yes,' Duggan agreed pleasantly, 'she did. From her somewhat limited point of view, of course.'

'He means the marriage angle,' Bert explained patiently to Ernest, somewhat in an Edgar Bergen fashion. 'He means her not knowing about it.'

Ernest looked at Duggan with the glassy eyes of a fighter who has just recently been pulped. 'I don't think I could make you understand.'

'Try.'

'You wouldn't by any chance be an only child?'

'No, there were eight of us kids,' Duggan said. 'Split fifty-fifty, boys and girls.'

'Then you wouldn't get it.'

'Get what?'

'The responsibility. Being limelighted from the moment when Dad passed on. You-are-now-the-man-of-the-family stuff. Being enveloped.' Ernest felt this wasn't strong enough and added, 'Being eaten, you might call it.'

'Play that again, will you?'

Ernest sank into silence and his gloom-drenched thoughts, and Bert took over.

'It's this way, Chief. What you see and what the world sees in Mrs. Dean is just the outside coat. A lot of polish and a lot of glitter. Well, that stuff is for the birds. The real woman, the inside woman, is and always has been strictly family. I mean as a wife to her husband and a mother to Ernest, and since the time her husband died of complicated pneumonia, it's been just Ernest. He is as hooked up to her as a Siamese twin, and you know what happens when you slice them apart.'

Just who, Duggan wondered, did Jackson think he was kidding? The answer was simple. Duggan. The thought of Mrs. Dean in the calm, wise role of a Whistler's Mother or in any closed-shop family situation was too much for Duggan to stomach. A vain, jealous, inordinately possessive and tyrannical woman seemed more like it. One with a strangle hold on her son. A death clutch.

'I'm still off the beam,' Duggan said.

'Tell me this, Mr. Dean, if you don't mind. Naturally you knew of your mother's thoughts on marriage. Did she expect you to stay single all your life?'

Flush deepened the bronze of Ernest's cheeks. Embarrassment? Duggan wondered. Or was it the anger of reluctant hate?

'Not all of my life, no, Mr. Duggan. Only for all of hers.'

'Still, you did get married.'

'When dead drunk.'

'Mr. Jackson — '

'Chief?'

'Isn't preventing anything of that nature a part of your responsibility?'

'Yes. But that night, Chief, was the night my sister died.'

'Bert was called to her bedside,' Ernest said. 'In Brooklyn. Me, I picked up Theda in a bar. Got tangled. Got married.'

Bert said, 'After Ernest told me she was throwing the hooks in him, I met her and did what I could to get him out of it — to keep it covered up while we bargained. For over two months now I've been sitting on the hatch.'

'What about this daybreak date, Mr.

Dean? Were you reaching an agreement?'

'Yes. It's what I had hoped.'

'Why make the appointment for daybreak?'

'It does sound sort of cloak-and-dagger, doesn't it? Theda wanted us to have it out last night, but I was tied up for dinner and dancing. I couldn't set any time for being back here.'

'You and Miss Spang? And, of course, Mr. Jackson?'

'Yes.'

'The three of you were together continuously?'

'We were,' Bert said, 'until Ernest and I turned in.'

'When was that?'

'Around three o'clock.'

'Do you have separate bedrooms?'

'Yes.'

'Mr. Dean, did you set an alarm clock for daybreak?'

'No. It would have waked up Mother. Bert woke me. He sat up and read.'

'Did Mr. Dean sleep all of the time, Mr. Jackson?'

'If you mean did he get up and leave

his room, he didn't. I could see his door from where I was sitting.'

So the watchdog had sat up and the watchdog had read. Had he, Duggan wondered, also napped? And if he had, during that straining stretch toward the break of day, were his eyes shut solely to the door of Ernest's bedroom? Were they not unable to observe a possible emergence of Mrs. Dean as well?

'Mr. Dean, I would like to get this absolutely clear, please. Until you went down to the beach you were to all purposes in somebody's company. You did go down to the beach alone, didn't you?'

'Yes.'

'For ten minutes? Fifteen?'

'About.'

'When you came upon your wife, what did you do to determine whether she was still alive? Or that help — resuscitation — would be useless?'

The question dropped with its hesitant fuse, and the bronze of Ernest's cheeks underwent a chalky fade.

'Theda was dead. I just knew it.'

'The dead are familiar to you?'

'No. My father — otherwise only Theda. And then I saw that Puerto Rican lady and got rattled. I guess you think I'm a pretty weak sister. I guess I am.'

'Most of us are at some time or other. Did you touch her?'

'Theda? God, no.'

'Well, let's spend a few minutes on her background. Her relatives, friends — what do you know about them?'

'Nothing.'

'Perhaps you do, Mr. Jackson? From your talks with her. While, as you say, you were holding down the hatch.'

Bert shrugged a pair of broad shoulders. 'She never said.'

'Then how did you contact her? Where did she live?'

'I didn't. She contacted me.'

'At the Deans'?'

'Yes. She would fix up the time and the place and we'd meet. Mostly it was a pizza joint in the West Forties.'

Duggan said to Ernest casually, 'Did you know that your wife was pregnant?'

'I didn't until last night. How did you know?'

'Medical examiner's report.'

'Last night when she stopped at the table for a minute while I was waiting for Jenny. She told me then.'

'She put the screws on,' Bert said and added, as though it explained everything and nothing further need be said about it, 'She was a tramp.'

* * *

Back in his bachelor quarters, which were an efficiency on the edge of town, Duggan tabulated the brief reports that had come through.

Miss Sangford's bathing cap had not been found.

Miss Sangford had a record and her prints were on file.

She had been booked twice. Once for attempted extortion, once on a badger-game charge.

For the past two years she had been living in her own small New York apartment in the East Fifties, ostensibly as a model but presumably, from the list of men's names and numbers in a book beside her telephone, as a call girl.

He picked up his phone and dialed Operator.

'It's Duggan, honey,' he said.

'Oh, hello, Bill.'

'Got a New York telephone directory handy?'

'Sure have.'

'Look up a number for me, will you please, honey?'

'Sure will, Bill. What name?'

He told her. He waited. She gave him a number. He did not bother to jot it down.

'Thanks, honey. Now get me Black's, will you?'

The connection with the motel made, he asked the clerk to connect him with the bar.

'Jimmy? Duggan here.'

'Hi, sleuth.'

'I need some dope on Sangford.'

'What kind?'

'Those two bottles of scotch last night. Did she often pull that?'

'Maybe two or three times, which is a pretty good record when you think about it. She was only here a week.'

'Was she a lush?'

'No more than most. She could hold it.'

'What about men? Did she play the field?'

'No. Young Dean exclusive. When any of the other fanged baboons tried to make her they never got off the plate. When are you going to pick him up, Sherlock?'

'Dean?'

'Who else?'

'You'd be amazed. Thanks, Jimmy. Be seeing you.'

'Why you clam-lipped — '

Duggan hung up.

He indulged in a satisfying, jaw-cracking yawn. Then he mused for a while on exactly how stupid a clever criminal could get.

★ ★ ★

The afternoon wore on, and gusty winds sent palm fronds streaming like a mad woman's hair. With sundown the cocktail lounge housed a jam to its last banquette, and Jimmy noted but few absentees from among the regulars. Mrs. Dean wasn't there, Jenny Spang and her mother weren't there, and Miss Fernandez was not there.

Miss Fernandez was in the living room of her apartment and was having a very tough time of it trying to make up her mind. What she wanted to do was to go to Mrs. Dean and warn her of the probability that danger of the most desperate character lay before her.

On this Miss Fernandez would have staked her reputation in San Juan as a woman with an uncanny gift for predicting the turn of things to come. Actually there was little of the uncanny about it and Miss Fernandez's forecasts were based on her sound deductive powers and the most elementary guideposts of common sense.

Finally, with a touch of grimness, Miss Fernandez opened the front door, braved the smash of wind around the pool's rim, and fought her way to the Dean corner unit. The expression on Mrs. Dean's face when she greeted her was one of very frank annoyance.

'Miss Fernandez? I know you will

understand and will forgive me if I do not ask you in. My nerves are in no condition to entertain guests.'

'I do not come here, Madame Dean, to be entertained. My mission is pressing. I have come to instruct you in a parable.'

Nothing could have been less fortunate than this opening remark. People did not 'instruct' Mrs. Dean. It was an operation she reserved for her exclusive use, and her temper invariably rose whenever, rarely, she was confronted with such an attitude on the part of another.

But Miss Fernandez did not budge. She raised a hand with two fingers extended upright in a gesture she had once observed Cardinal Filipe Hernandos employ in the face of a recalcitrant penitent.

'It is my unshakable purpose,' she said simply, 'to save your life.'

Against her better judgment, Mrs. Dean did feel her curiosity being aroused.

'Let's get in out of this typhoon,' she said, 'and then you can tell me about it.'

In the living room, in the comparative quiet induced by closed jalousies, Miss Fernandez detoured toward the point.

'There was once,' she said, 'a fish.'

Mrs. Dean clenched her fingers. 'Please, let's keep it simple, will you? No fish.'

'A fish,' Miss Fernandez went on inexorably, 'who was in residence in a coral palace at the bottom of the deep, deep sea. It was, this fish, a monster and with a monster's appetite that it had trouble in satisfying because it was totally blind.'

'Look. This is perfectly fascinating but I simply have not got the strength — '

'Patience, madame! One discloses another fish, equally monstrous but blessed with two baby eyes.'

Mrs. Dean stood up. This fantastic rubbish was not only ridiculous but galling, and she intended to put an end to it. Apart from herself being clearly cast as the monstrous blind horror in the tale, the second fish was undoubtedly intended to represent her son. Unquestionably the woman was mad. There was that distinct look of introverted passion in her dark accusing eyes.

'I must ask you to leave me,' she said. 'Go, please — at once — I am not well — '

Disconcertingly, entirely unexpectedly, Miss Fernandez burst into tears, which poured from deep, shaken sobbing. It was certainly the last thing that Mrs. Dean had expected, and she said rather stupidly, 'I shall get you a glass of water.'

She went into the service pantry and found that the pitcher of chilled water was empty. So she broke out ice cubes, with the usual time and bother that that job entails. It was several minutes before she returned to the living room with the water, only to find Miss Fernandez gone and, oddly, like a clever magical trick, Mrs. Spang standing there in her place.

'That Puerto Rican woman let me in, dear. Then she positively swam past me in a flood of tears and went out. Is she quite sane? At times I've wondered. And the weirdest thing — she kept muttering between sobs, blind, blind. Then something about danger and the foolish one not listening.'

'She has some silly idea that my life is in danger. Of course she is crazy. She ought to be committed.'

Little muscles in Mrs. Spang's face

tensed, giving her expression the quality of a plaster mask.

'Your — life, dear?'

'Yes. Apparently I am a monstrous fish at the bottom of the sea, eating everything in sight even though I'm blind as a bat.'

'Are you serious? She really said things like that?'

'She did. She simply barged in, and I could do nothing to stop her gibbering.'

'But how utterly weird. You don't suppose — '

'Suppose what?'

'No, no, it's too absurd. That she could have second sight, or extrasensory perception as they call it? Like those frightening tests and things going on at Duke University? Something about blindfolds and colored cards.'

Mrs. Dean said with a venom so sharp that the words sank into Mrs. Spang like little knives, 'If any colored cards or rabbits are going to be pulled out of a hat — I intend to pull them.'

The plaster look set more rigidly until it seemed that when Mrs. Spang moved her lips her skin would crack.

'My dear, you look so intense. I simply don't follow you.'

Mrs. Dean laughed unmusically. 'They say that patience is a virtue. Fools! It's the most valuable weapon that exists.'

'Weapon?'

'Yes, weapon. And I intend to employ it to the hilt.'

'Dear — is it possible — I mean, do you know something?'

'About the drowning of that despicable harlot?' Mrs. Dean looked levelly at Mrs. Spang for a long moment, dissecting with a surgeon's touch those particles of avarice and tigerish rapacity which lay beneath the woman's creamed and tinted skin. She said, 'What do you think?'

★   ★   ★

Mrs. Dean was a shaken woman. The world, her world, where she had lived with every assurance of dependable continuance, had exploded in her face. She loved her son. Of that there could be no doubt. And all of her restrictions upon his freedom were not, as she saw them,

62

restrictions at all but rather a constant imposition of wise guidance.

The diseased nature of the intensity of ownership that she felt about Ernest did not occur to her ever, and she honestly believed that everything she did was for his good.

And who better than herself could shelter him with this sturdy umbrella against the dangerous storms of life? Certainly not a child like Jenny, especially with her type of covetous, fortune-hunting mother like Mrs. Spang. No, Jenny couldn't — no more than could the other ones have. What had been their names — Estelle? Marguerite? That rather dangerous one — Ethel?

Squashed. All of them. Buglike, beneath a diamond-studded heel.

Then this.

The unbelievable treachery of a secret wife.

A dead one, now.

Murdered.

Her features hardened. There was a debt connected with murder. The guilty paid it and sometimes, rarely, the innocent. Had it been a mistake to let the affair go so far? She caught herself up. It was her false knowledge that had betrayed her, because from all she had known about it, the Sangford menace had only existed during the past week.

Mrs. Dean had never felt like this before, with her mental faculties fractured into violent shards that were nothing but meaningless strays of thoughts. Certainly she had never felt so miserable, so downright sick at heart and all straight through. Nor so sweaty chill with ice-cold anger.

She noticed without much interest that the time was an hour after midnight. It would be several hours more before Ernest and Bert would return from Mario's gambling club on the county line. She had insisted upon Ernest's going, as she wanted him to follow the regular pattern of his evenings, to flaunt his unconcern in the face of a solidifying public opinion that was so outrageously unjust.

Her sigh was an exclamation point, as sharp as a stiletto of Damascus steel. There would be justice, yes. But it was she who would deal it out.

Mrs. Dean seldom drank alone but she felt the need of a sustaining jolt right now. A good stiff gin and tonic. In the service pantry it occurred to her as odd that only one bottle of tonic water should be in the refrigerator. She could distinctly recall that earlier in the day there had been three. Neither Ernest nor Bert ever drank tonic water, disliking its bitterish quinine flavor. Possibly the maid? A Bahama Negress with British tastes?

She dropped ice cubes in a tall glass and poured a double shot of gin. The cap of the tonic water did not, for once, stick as though it had been soldered on. It came off quite easily under the first leverage of the bottle opener. She stirred the drink and carried it, untasted, back toward the living room, pausing in the short dark hallway to close the beach door which the wind apparently had blown open.

She decided that the living room lounge would be the proper setting for her discovery by Ernest upon his return. She would be found lying there in a dead faint as a result of a severe attack of the heart, brought on by his unspeakable act of deceit. From there she would proceed to the matter of Jenny Spang.

She placed the gin and tonic on a table before the lounge, sat down, and then reached for her handbag, which was lying against an end pillow, a place where she generally tossed it on returning to the apartment. She rummaged through its contents for the vial of strychnine tablets which, conspicuously placed upon the table, would bear mute testimony to the mortal shock she had suffered.

She became aware that the vial was empty.

She sat motionless while an arctic cold embraced every fraction of her body and while her eyes, with a dreadful speculation, traveled toward and rested on the glass that contained the gin and tonic water.

The single bottle where there had been three, and the cap that had flipped off with a flick!

How terribly, terribly clever, she thought. What could better conceal the bitter taste of strychnine than the bitter flavor of quinine? They were so much akin that it would be difficult to tell them apart. Gently her hand reached out. Gently, experimentally, she sipped, allowing the liquid globules of the drink to spread upon her tongue.

Then, abruptly, she spat them out.

Was it the confusion of horrific belief that made the bitterness seem unusually acute? A conviction that the contents of the glass contained liquid death? Curiosity once had caused her to ask her doctor what a death from strychnine poisoning would be like. She recalled that the symptoms began about ten or fifteen minutes after administering — a premonition of impending calamity, a shuddering, a sudden violent tetanic spasm, a stiff sardonic grin, and (this disturbed Mrs. Dean more than anything else) the mentality of the victim during those convulsions usually remained clear.

How did it end? That moment when death blasted you smack out of life — yes, she remembered now. It crushed you into its skeleton oblivion either from exhaustion or, in the midst of a paroxysm, from asphyxia.

Mrs. Dean replaced the glass upon the

table beside the empty vial.

Oddly, she felt fresh-born. Had others felt so too? Others who were given, as she was, a second chance to keep on living through the coming generous years? Really — so close had been her brush with it — to return from the dead to life.

There was no question in her mind whatever but that the bottle of tonic water had been loaded with a lethal dose of strychnine and then recapped. That the other two remembered bottles had been disposed of so that there would be no choice. And no one but herself was accustomed to use the tonic, a matter of common knowledge to any of the regulars who patronized the bar, as were the ever-present tablets of strychnine for use in the event of a sudden heart attack.

The empty vial? Why had it not been disposed of too? But of course. It had purposely been left to be found as a grim signpost that in her shock and heart-wrenching disillusion over the beastly Sangford marriage situation she had taken her own life.

Mrs. Dean entered upon her second

emotional phase, having now finished with the exaltation of still being alive. Like a dark tide within her rushed the full surge of the vengeance that would be hers. She wondered what the death penalty was in Florida and felt pretty certain that it was the electric chair.

Her first thought was to preserve the drink as evidence. It was indicative of her shaken state of mind that she failed to realize that the trial would be held for the willful drowning of Theda Sangford and not for this unsuccessful attempted homicide upon herself.

The lazy minutes of the clock had moved to one-fifteen.

She returned to the service pantry and fished the empty tonic-water bottle and its cap from the garbage can. Among the utensils in a drawer she located a funnel. These things she carried back into the living room and set them on the empty coffee table.

Empty —

Her electrified look raked its surface. The drink and the strychnine vial were gone. The cold of her anger was replaced by a clammy sweat of fright. The beach door which so recently she had closed — it was not the wind that had blown it open. Not originally. Not until in an excess of stealth the intruder had failed to shut it securely after creeping inside from the outer night.

Mrs. Dean's dread reached its saturation point as she realized that her reactions to finding the strychnine vial empty had been observed by this intruder, and it must be obvious that the nipped poison attempt would boomerang into exposure and arrest. Frightened almost to the point of nausea, she wondered whether this glorious pulse of living, which but so briefly had seemed secured, was crashing back into jeopardy.

A switch clicked, dousing the lights and numbing Mrs. Dean within a paralyzing darkness that froze the vocal muscles with which, in her extremity, she wished to scream. A timeless moment of graveyard hush was broken only by twin breathings, one of which was her own.

The curved fingers of a strangler clamped about her throat.

* * *

Miss Fernandez, from her observation post at a jalousie in her own living room, saw the living room blinds of the Dean apartment go dark. She noted the time by her wrist watch: one twenty-three. A feeling of foreboding had held her at this vigil during the past half hour, and no one had either entered the Dean apartment or left. Not by the front door. There was, Miss Fernandez reflected, the door that opened on the beach.

Her dour thoughts were confirmed when the Venetian blinds of Mrs. Dean's bedroom failed to indicate that lamps had been turned on in order that Mrs. Dean might retire. She looked at her wrist watch again and saw that five minutes had passed. Mrs. Dean would not prepare to retire in the dark. This Miss Fernandez considered to be a purely academic deduction.

Her thoughts phrased themselves in the stilted elegance of early Latin-American drama. Something was amiss. Her rebuff earlier in the evening at the hands of Mrs.

Dean had been a severe one, and it was with the greatest strength of character that she forced herself to face a further ordeal. She threw a velvet stole about her shoulders as a shield against the chill night wind and made her way around the swimming pool's rim.

There was no answer to the chime. Miss Fernandez opened the front door and stepped into the pitch-darkness of the room. As she had expected, the light switch was similarly placed to her own. She pressed it, flooding the scene with amber.

Mrs. Dean's body lay tossed on the carpeting near the lounge. A tongue tip protruded. The eyes gave an unpleasant impression of dropping from their sockets. The face was a dusky blue.

Miss Fernandez touched a wrist. The flesh was warm. She felt for and found no pulse. A mirror of her compact held against the nostrils remained unclouded. They were simple tests and definitely inconclusive, but they were the only ones which Miss Fernandez knew.

She was completely calm. Her nerves, from having so many times faced it, were immune to a violent death. She wished to get in touch with Chief Duggan and to have things remain exactly as they were until he got there. To accomplish this meant avoiding the furor that would follow putting a call through the front-office switchboard.

From a strong draft in the hallway she imagined the beach door would be open. It was, and she left it so and went to the telephone booth attached to Oscar Bjorgsen's beach-wear shop. With the glow from a cigarette lighter she looked up the number and dialed.

'Chief Duggan?'

'Yes?'

'It is Loreta Fernandez who speaks.'

'Yes, Miss Fernandez?'

'It concerns Mrs. Dean. She is choked dead.'

Duggan took the news in one admirable stride. 'Where are you?'

'The telephone cubicle of the lifeguard. You would wish things to be untouched. I am not unversed in the police aspects of crime. The motel switchboard, you understand?'

'Is she in her apartment?'

'Yes.'

'You did the right thing. Tell me, can you stand going back? Maybe wait in the patio until I get there?'

'I shall permit no one to enter until you come.'

'Ten minutes, then.'

Oddly, Miss Fernandez then said, 'There is no rush. I think we both know that.'

She hung up, and Duggan had the strong impression that in her peculiarly melodramatic and witchcraft fashion she had determined the identity of the killer and the motive for the crimes. And this knowledge, he thought with a good touch of grimness, was about as safe to cart around as a Molotov cocktail, especially in view of Miss Fernandez's publicized habit of groping for things in mists.

Before leaving his quarters he put through a call to Dr. Sibley. 'Frank? This is Duggan.'

'Oh yes, Bill?'

'Another one. Mrs. Dean. Strangled.'

'At Black's?'

'Yes, in her apartment. When you've done what you have to there, there's something I need, and I need it bad. The Gettler test on Sangford. Can you jump the gun on that?'

Sibley counted hours.

'Well, the solutions have been standing thirteen, fourteen hours. I guess possibly.'

'Thanks, Frank.'

'I'll do my best, Bill.'

Duggan hung up, only to dial again several times, making the regular arrangements — Roth to take pictures, a technician for fingerprints, and Officer Day, whom he picked up and drove with him toward Black's.

Day, of course, had the job wrapped up. 'It's as plain as the nose on your face, Chief.'

'Let's not get personal, Pinkerton.'

'It's so plain it falls into slots. Like pinballs. Secret wife — I am speaking now of Sangford.'

'That I gathered.'

'Both her plus unwanted child stashed for good on ice, and the field all clear to gather in the Spang number in a legal marriage with the exception of one thing.'

'Mama.'

'Exactly right. We were pin-pointed heads not to case her as the next on the list.'

Duggan said with a deadly seriousness, 'We weren't. I was.'

'I kept saying we should have nabbed him, Gettler test or no Gettler test. Didn't I?'

'You did.'

'So now he gives his watchdog the slip and chokes to death the last hurdle to his happiness. How long does it take to choke, Chief?'

'Depends. Usually less than a few minutes, from the effects of asphyxia, cerebral anemia, and shock.'

'No kidding! I had it taped as simply lack of wind.'

'A lush, if he's hitting it, gets it quicker and with less bother. With mugging, the victim can kick off at any time from shock while struggling, even before asphyxia is complete.'

'I wouldn't line Mrs. Dean up as a lush, would you?'

'No, I'd figure her for a good stiff fight. I want you to get the scrapings from her fingernails and give them to Sibley. He'll know what to do with them.'

'You figure she raked him?'

'Probably. May have gouged the wrists, backs of the hands. Usually there's a sign.' Duggan sheered abruptly, 'What do you know about the lifeguard? Jergson? Bjorgsen?'

'Oscar?'

'Yes, Oscar.'

'He is hell on skirts. Right now he's playing a blond number from Vero Beach who's curb-hopping at Hank's drive-in and — '

' — and her husband is sending him mash notes from the Ku Klux Klan.'

'Gee, Chief, how did you know?'

'I get around. And I'm not interested in his love life. What I want to know is can you depend on him? Can he keep his trap shut?'

'About his morals, Chief, I wouldn't know.'

'No matter. I'll find out myself.'

'Why?'

'Got a job I want him to do.' They drew up in the motels parking lot. 'I'm going to turn the routine over to you. Stick in the Dean apartment and, when the boys come, roll it.'

'Where will you be, Chief?'

'I'll be around.'

★　★　★

After looking at the body and implanting in his mind a photographic impression of the living room and other quarters of the apartment, which occupied him little more than a matter of minutes, Duggan left Day in charge and then joined Miss Fernandez in the patio.

The wind had tapered to a stiffish breeze and stars were developing in the sky. The entrance light was on, and its glow washed yellowly over the bougain-villea and the trimmed hibiscus hedge that separated the unit's patio from the patio of the Spangs. It touched with saffron the high complexion of Miss Fernandez's dusky cheeks and added an almost catlike glow to her somber brown eyes.

'What was it really caused you to come over here?' he asked.

'As I announced in our initial brevity, the lights. They went out. No others came on.'

'This premonition of' — Duggan sought the word she had used — 'of amissness, was there nothing more definite?'

'What would one wish? The lights in a salon go out. The lights in a boudoir do not turn on. No lights turn on. No person departs. Not, one says, by the front door. One specifies a door in the rear to the beach, left open when the killer in a frenzy fled.'

'Miss Fernandez, I don't want to force the point, but I want you to think back during that half hour when you told me you were watching. Was there nothing, no incident, no matter how trifling, that you can remember?'

A slight quiver skimmed the expanses of her body as the fact struck home that Duggan, deliberately and with considerable obviousness, had winked. There was no doubt about it. Miss Fernandez clutched back through her memory of U.S. crime procedure as she had culled it from the paperback translations. More than once a smart detective had tipped a witness that their conversation was being overheard, usually by some mechanical device concealed behind a picture or in a potted plant. Was this deliberate wink such a tip?

She thought it was. Her gaze traveled casually about the patio, dwelt less casually on the hibiscus hedge on the other side of which was the patio of Mrs. Spang, the desperate mother who was making her last stand.

The significance of the wink became plainer still. It not alone indicated the probability of eavesdropping ears, but it invited co-operation as well. Surely an affirmation of the question Duggan had just asked. Being both at heart and by national temperament a plotter of great aplomb, she seized on this role of undercover conspirator with a pleasurable gusto.

There was a standardized pattern for the setup, and she followed it.

'All, now that I reflect — '

A brief smile assured her that she was on the right track.

She continued, 'It is — how can I express it to you? A something delicate as a shadow — '

Duggan suggested helpfully, 'In a mist?'

'A mist, yes. Very black. Right now this thing eludes, but it will come back. Perhaps the subconscious while I repose. Perhaps by dawning.'

'Perhaps like yesterday morning around daybreak, when you make a practice of taking a dip and picking up shells?'

'But of course! Always it is at dawning when thoughts are best.' She added darkly and apparently just for the hell of it, 'When the waters cool.'

Duggan cut her short, having gained his point. At least he hoped he had, felt pretty sure of it. He couldn't come right out and say: Set yourself up as a sitting duck. But that was what he meant, and he believed that Miss Fernandez understood. If he had judged her correctly she would go through with the job with stubborn courage.

'I'm going to the bar,' he said. 'I want to try and locate young Dean.'

He walked away, out of the yellow light and into the dark with its descending wind. Miss Fernandez moved close to the hibiscus hedge and said softly, experimentally, 'Madame Spang?'

Something like a whimper answered. Then the faded face of Mrs. Spang was rising like a cobweb moon across the hedge and saying, 'I'm worried stiff. She shouldn't have gone off that way.'

'One does not select the manner of one's ultimate departure.'

'I don't mean Mrs. Dean. I mean Jenny. Quite a while ago — several hours ago. She said she was running over to the cocktail lounge for a while to watch television. I finally got so worried I went in search of her. Jimmy and Francine both said she hadn't been there at all. She's gone. Just gone.'

Miss Fernandez asked quietly, 'How is it that you are aware of Mrs. Dean's death?'

'It's because I've been sitting here worrying and I saw you come over and go in and light the light. I looked in through

82

a jalousie, and it was ghastly — horrible. And now on top of it, Jenny.'

'Madame, you have my sympathy. Do not concern yourself about that lovely child. She goes with God.'

'It's all very well for you to say so. But I tell you I'm weak. Just sick and weak.'

'A drink?'

'Yes. You'll come with me?'

'That is a certainty, Madame Spang.'

★   ★   ★

'I'm telling you,' Jimmy said to Duggan, 'that's all I know. Dean and Jackson shoved off for Mario's about nine to try and get even, and they haven't been back here again. Mrs. Spang tottered in around an hour ago and buzzed Francine and me.

'Did we know where dear Jenny was? Had we — Say, get a load of who's just coming in, Bill. Old Faithful Jackson and with no sonny boy in tow. He looks like an uncooked pancake.'

Jackson rather did, with his deep tan drained by tiredness or worry into a pasty gray. He came directly over to the bar and to Duggan and said, 'I lost him.'

'At Mario's?'

'Yes. Is it true what that guy outside said? She's dead?'

'Yes.'

'Choked?'

'Yes.'

'When?'

'Not long,' Duggan said.

'I ought to take three whiskies as fast as I can put them away.'

'Why?'

'It's not good. That's why.'

'When did Dean skip?'

'Maybe around ten. He went up to Mario's office to get him to cash a check. Mario did and left him there finishing a drink. When he got back, Ernest was gone, and Mario figured he was down bucking the wheel.'

'Ten was almost four hours ago, Jackson.'

'I know it.'

'It's a long time to look.'

'It's a long town, beach, and county. I covered every joint we've ever been to.'

'In what?'

'What do you mean in what?'

'Didn't he take his car? I should have thought he would.'

'No. I figure he high-tailed it with some digger or new-found buddy-buddy or took a cab. He's been lifting them all day, and believe me it's been one tough day.'

'Of course you checked back here?'

'You think I'm crazy, Chief? Would I want Mrs. Dean to know I'd let him get slopped up and give me the slip? He's so fouled up you can't tell what he'll do.'

'One thing I guess we can bank on. Sons just don't kill their mothers.'

Jimmy leaned further across the bar and stuck in an interested oar. 'But,' he informed them, 'sometimes they do kill their wives.'

'That tramp?' Jackson said disgustedly. 'You're in a cloud, brother. Ernest wouldn't kill a fly. It's just that at times he blacks out and could maybe start swimming to China for all we'd know. You going to check with Mario, Chief?'

'Yes.'

'Maybe you can get something out of

him. When I kept pestering him he gave me the baby-blue-eyes runaround. 'No,' he says, 'I have no idea what could have happened to Mr. Dean. Why don't you earn your dough and go look?' Then actually he titters. The clammy jerk.'

Miss Fernandez and Mrs. Spang came into the lounge, and Mrs. Spang spotted Bert Jackson. The two women headed toward them, and Duggan eased away, giving Miss Fernandez the faint lowering of a left eyelid and getting a jolt to find her giving him back the same.

Lights were on in Oscar Bjorgsen's quarters of the beach-wear shop. Duggan knocked and, being called to come in, found himself facing a typical Norse giant, currently attired in a lime shanting sport shirt and dark gray slacks.

'Bjorgsen?'

'Yes. You're Chief Duggan?'

'Yes. I want to use the phone booth for a few minutes, then I'd like a talk.'

Bjorgsen looked at an expensive wrist watch that told, to his constant bewilderment, the day, the month, and the phases of the moon as bonuses to the time. It was a gift from an appreciative coal baroness from Pittsburgh.

'Glad to, Chief. She'll wait.'

'Vero Beach?'

'That's right. What do we talk about? Sangford? Mrs. Dean?'

'In a way.'

'Boy, is this crib getting loused up with stiffs.'

Duggan agreed and, going to the outside phone booth, shut himself in, looked up a private number in a small notebook, and dialed.

A pleasant young woman's voice said, 'Mario's Club Continental.'

'Duggan speaking. Police chief, Halycon.'

'Oh yes, Chief?'

'I'd like to talk with Mario. About young Dean. His mother has just been killed.'

'Oh no! I mean it's so terrible always, you just never can get used to it. Please wait a minute, Chief.'

Duggan waited.

A well-polished voice said, 'Chief Duggan? I am Mario. Did I get it straight about Mrs. Dean?'

'Yes. Strangled.'

'When?'

'Maybe an hour ago. Maybe more or less.'

'Then that is okay.'

'An alibi for Dean?'

'Yes.'

'You're dead sure?'

'Nobody can be dead sure, Chief. If so, I would be out of business. I do know Dean called me up around that time and said he was keeping the car all night. He said he was calling from Palm Beach.'

'What about this car?'

'I will tell you. He came to my office around ten. I cashed a check for a thousand. I keep some on hand for the convenience of my guests. He asked to borrow a car for several hours.'

'Why didn't he use his own?'

'It was his wish to evade Mr. Jackson.'

'Why?'

'He did not say. He told me very little. In fact, he told me nothing, and I did not inquire. He asked me to clam up about the car, so when Mr. Jackson blew his top I made with the old double. Mr. Dean is too valuable a customer.'

'This car — a Caddy convertible, '58, I suppose?'

Mario laughed agreeably. 'What else would you expect? Black, white-walls, and a lemon top. No neon lights.'

'Would you have the license number?'

Mario consulted a notebook containing the club's less vital statistics and gave Duggan a number.

'There was also this,' he said. 'No matter what he was up to, I figured the kid needed a break. That mother of his was keeping him in Alcatraz and, speaking impersonally, I am glad that she is cooked.'

Duggan thanked Mario and hung up. He put through several calls arranging for a statewide general on the car for all patrols and the several night disk jockeys, requesting that Ernest Dean be in turn requested to contact Chief Duggan at Blacks. The nature of the request: Urgent.

He dialed Tropical. He asked to be connected with Dr. Sibley.

Sibley said shortly, 'Bill?'

'Yes, Frank. Any luck?'

'Plenty. Mr. Gettler's test is all done, and successfully too. You were absolutely right. And to that fact, under oath, will I so testify in court. What makes you so smart?'

'I just happen to know floaters, that's all. I was a lifeguard for a while.'

'Even so. That might account for your build but not for your brains.'

'You've got the boys all wrong,' Duggan said. 'Catch one with clothes on, and he'll slap a Phi Beta Kappa key in your face. Anything yet on Mrs. Dean?'

'Haven't started. But those fingernail scrapings — courtesy of Officer Day — I've examined them microscopically. Not chemically as yet. No flesh. No blood. Just some rubber.'

'Rubber?'

'That's right, Bill. Red rubber. Like from rubber gloves such, I suggest to your eagle-hawk mind, as women use when they dye their hair.'

'What's an eagle hawk?'

'Do we care?'

'No.'

'Did Mrs. Dean dye her hair?' Sibley asked. 'I've yet to look.'

'Sure she did, but with her dough she

didn't do it in rubber gloves. It was done in a box seat at some Emile's or Antoine's.' But, Duggan thought reflectively, the down-to-her-last-nickel Mrs. Spang would do her own hair dyeing.

'I told you that you were a bright boy,' Sibley said. 'When do you ring up the curtain on the final act?'

'Maybe around daybreak. Maybe.'

'Well, good hunting to you.'

'Thanks, Frank. I'll save the fox's tail for your handlebars.'

Duggan hung up. Goodbye, he thought, to any scratches on the strangler's hands and wrists. Rubber gloves came well up on the forearm. For a short while he stood watching the pale line of combers crash and cream, hissing, on the sand. They had movement in the circumscribed arena of this private world where nothing else moved at all. Only the wind, which you could hear and feel but could not see.

In his mind's eye he projected a picture of the coming daybreak, of a lone figure in her swim suit of flamingo, bravely defenseless in all this emptiness, with eyes cast sandward in a search for shells. And then, from the lips of the murderer, the casual invitation for a mutual swim.

He returned to Bjorgsen's quarters.

He said, 'Look, Bjorgsen. Here's what I'd like for us to do.'

He outlined his plan and thus set in motion one of the most unpredictable boners of his official existence.

The motel slept, and the slow minutes paced on. The units were dark in this sleep with the exception of the living-room jalousies of the Deans'.

Duggan went in and was pleased to notice that the body had been taken away. He gave a moment of audience appreciation to the duet of gurgles and snores that were being broadcast from Station Day, who slouched almost flat in a lounge chair, and from the room where Bert Jackson lay entirely flat on his bed.

Careful not to alarm the watchdogs by barking and waking them up, Duggan quietly cased the room in greater detail than he had before. This careful search disclosed an all but unnoticeable tip of metal projecting from under the front fringe of the lounge. It was a funnel, and, with respectful regard for fingerprints, he placed it on the coffee table.

The thing was incongruous, especially its location from having rolled or been kicked beneath the lounge, and the incongruous always intrigued him. What was the funnel used for? To pour something into something through the neck of a bottle. Duggan, he congratulated himself, you are quick as a whippet. The funnels size seemed about right for a beer bottle or one for soft drinks.

He pursued the puzzle into the service pantry. Apparently no answer there. He rooted around and found a plastic vegetable bag, got the funnel, bagged it, and stashed it behind china on the shelf of a wall cabinet. He went on with his casing against the continued mood music of snores.

★ ★ ★

The hours rolled, and the wind sank from stiff to breeze, and the anger went hugely out of the ocean, and its movement, with the exception of an occasional mutinous kick-up, grew smooth, like a strong sleeper's chest.

The night still held, but the feel of dawn was in the air, and Miss Fernandez prepared. She deliberately advertised her awakening by turning on both bedroom and living room lights. Then she knelt and said her morning prayers. They included a request that God, through the offices of Chief Duggan, would so arrange her prospects that she might view again her beloved San Juan, her beloved fishing villages on the south coast and little mountain hamlets in the heart of Puerto Rico's coffee country, and her favorite 'out-on-the-island' spots of Ponce, Parguera, Mayaguez, and Coamo.

Having finished up this comprehensive Cook's Tour, she exchanged her nightdress for the flamingo swim suit. From the cutlery drawer in the service pantry she selected a small paring knife and satisfied herself as to its point and cutting edge. She was, with knives, in the nature of a connoisseur. She dropped it into the bag she carried for shells.

Darkness receded to the thin spread of

pre-dawn and, as the moment approached, became zero hour near, Miss Fernandez experienced a tension of the little nerves. This was in no manner connected with any heart-restrictive qualities of fear (such as had held the screams unborn in the throat of Mrs. Dean), for she was content that Duggan would never have advanced his semi-subtle suggestion, to speak of it kindly, without having proper guards for her safety in mind.

The tension was rather that of a prima donna awaiting the cue to bring her on stage, and a band of pale raspberry in the eastern sky warned her that the cue had come. She turned out lights, then stepped into the pastel hush of the patio, and it seemed that she alone in the world was awake, but she knew this was not so.

Unless Duggan's calculations and her own were at serious fault, the killer, at this moment masked behind some aspect of nature or the structural jobs of man, would already be giving her the lethal eye.

She walked leisurely past the black pearl surface of the swimming pool and toward the vaulted passageway leading to the beach. Its tiled flooring was glassy cool, and then the sand was beneath her feet and carpeted before her to the creamy sheet of foam as each comber spent its journey on the shale. She eyed the surf professionally, being an excellent swimmer, and thought it moderate, neither dabble-flat nor undertow-strong.

Miss Fernandez crossed the dry section pitted with the footprints of yesterday and as yet unraked for the morning, and came to the table-top firmness of the moist, packed shelf, clean-washed by the tide on ebb.

She assumed the familiar pose, the slight stoop and the downcast look of the seeker after shells. But her eyes were blind, and such few specimens as she gathered were worthless ones picked up for effect at random. She had reached the northern limit of Black's private beach when she sensed (certainly it was impossible to hear footfalls on the sand) the presence of someone behind her.

'Good morning,' the voice said pleasantly.

She permitted the bag of shells to drop and then fumbled for it clumsily, but before she could retrieve it it was picked up.

'So sorry, Miss Fernandez. I hope I didn't startle you. Although obviously I must have.'

She smiled noncommittally. 'One is so accustomed to isolation at this hour.'

'After that ghastly business of last night I thought an early dip might be bracing.'

She shopped for a platitude. 'Sleep is difficult during moments of drama.'

'Impossible, I found it. Although we often think we've stayed awake through the night, when actually we've napped.'

She wondered for how long this prattle would slide on with the balance of a tightrope walker before the hands would initiate their blunt purpose, which was to kill her, to silence her for good.

At the moment the hands were fumbling with the bag of shells, pressing the contents exploratively through the denim cloth, and pausing (Miss Fernandez could tell the precise instant) when they identified the shape and substance of the paring knife. Then the bag was tossed carelessly down on the sand.

'Let's take a plunge, Miss Fernandez. Shall we?'

'If you wish.'

Strongly fatalistic by nature, Miss Fernandez glanced fractionally at the shell bag, humped now so uselessly with its improvised stiletto on the beach.

Companionably they walked, two people alone on this plateau of emptiness that embraced the sands and the surface of the sea and the sky above. A broken wave hissed swift along the shelf. It curled with spent force past their ankles, warm and clean and sharp in this remainder of its former power. They dove through a roller that crested in, emerged into the long smooth troughs and moderate hills, and swam out to the flatter heave.

They stopped for a breather, treading water, and Miss Fernandez kept, with the careless motion of her arms, a wary space between.

'You swim well, Mr. Jackson,' she said.

'Almost as well as you do.' Bert's eyes turned beachward and found it devoid of life. But you never knew. He gauged the dawn. Pretty bright by now. And soon the sun. 'I think we've come out far enough,' he said. 'Don't you?'

Several yards from where the feet of Bert and Miss Fernandez were treading water, and at a slightly lower level, Duggan and Bjorgsen observed the lazy paddlings from their submerged retreat. They were equipped with aqualungs, weighted belts, flippers, and masks from the skin-diving stock of the beach-wear shop.

The light was strong enough for good vision, sifting down through the ocean ceiling of opalescent amber-grays. As Bert's legs drifted with barely perceptible purpose closer to the legs of Miss Fernandez, both men, with fishlike ease, came closer too.

Duggan was an immeasurably relieved man. The situation was well in hand. Two witnesses, himself and Bjorgsen, would apprehend the killer in his third and last attack upon a human life. His admiration for Miss Fernandez knew no bounds.

Gently between the two sets of dangling legs, gently the gap decreased.

Now the legs of Bert were quite still, and whipcord muscles tensed along their thighs until, with the power crash of a barracuda, Bert dove and, grasping Miss Fernandez by her ankles, yanked her below.

Not unlike a barracuda himself, Duggan struck.

In addition to his muscular strength Duggan had the tremendous advantage of shock-tactic surprise. Bert had no conceivable way of knowing what it was that had hit him, and his first impression was that the arm that lashed around his throat, mugging him, was the tentacle of an octopus. He instantly gave up his intentions regarding Miss Fernandez and panicked into a violent effort to shed the stranglehold of this monster of the deep.

While this was going on, Bjorgsen had gripped and surfaced with Miss Fernandez, when he threw back his mask and asked solicitously, 'Are you okay?'

Miss Fernandez discarded a final mouthful of salt water. Although still a little confused over the incredible rescue by this goggled creature (now identified), she felt as strong as an ox and quite generally fine.

'A little damp inside, Mr. Bjorgsen.

Otherwise okay. But Mr. Duggan — he is, one gathers, below? Should we not create a diversion? Assist?'

'Why?' Oscar asked reasonably. 'Unless they surface by the next ten seconds that Jackson crumb will be a windless cadaver. Duggan's got a 'lung. One thing — '

'Yes?'

'Jackson. His being the killer. To me it don't make sense.'

'You will find, Mr. Bjorgsen, that when the evidence and motive for these tragedies are disclosed — the greed, the lust, the knives of fear, the repressions of a caste-hungry soul — it is the only solution that does.'

Duggan's masked head broke water first. Then Bert's sullen good looks emerged too, only to have his jaw get a knockout crash from Duggan's fist.

Duggan unmasked. 'You two all right?' he asked.

'Tops, Chief,' Oscar said.

'Stick together. I'll tow this squid ashore.'

They offered an uneventful flotilla-in-quartet on their passage toward the beach. Uneventful, that is, until they struck the line of surf when, towering in its comparative magnitude up behind them, a seventh wave barreled in at express speed.

Duggan's reaction to this ever-unpredictable phenomenon of the sea was to find himself upended and his face slammed with piston force down into the ocean floor, while his tow, the flaccid Bert, became galvanized into a dynamo and, with a forceful kick in the small of Duggan's back, broke loose. The inescapable confusion of the moment held the tumbling uncertainties of earthquake.

Being unencumbered with aqualungs, weighted belts, and flippers, Bert easily struggled ashore before any of the others got a nose or an eye out of water. He wasted no time but sprinted for the vaulted beach archway, vanishing into its cavern while the rest were still recovering their strength and wits.

Having finally disentangled herself from Oscar, Miss Fernandez battled the resurgent undertow's pull and waded ashore. Duggan and Bjorgsen followed.

'Where is he?' Oscar asked.

The three looked, breathing heavily, at

Bert's last known place of residence — the surf.

'Better see what we can do,' Duggan said, starting to shed his skin-diving paraphernalia.

Bjorgsen followed suit, and they were on the point of taking a running plunge when Miss Fernandez called their attention to the footprints in the sand.

'That,' she said, indicating the deep, sharp impacts in the smooth-washed shale, 'is the direction in which he went.'

★ ★ ★

Dawn by now was in full force, and Bert had what he felt to be the most incredible stroke of good luck. He had pounded at lung-bursting speed through the arched vault and then on toward the parking lot of the motel. He had no thought beyond instant flight and an urge to put as much distance as he could between himself and the law until he could devise some scheme for a more permanent escape.

It was his intention to use the Jaguar, Ernest's car, which Bert had parked on his after-midnight return. A spare ignition key was always cached with a magnetized gadget under a fender. He had about reached it when a red Pontiac convertible flashed into the parking lot and headed for an open space alongside the Jaguar. To his confused amazement Bert saw that Jenny Spang was driving it and that Ernest, apparently blotto and out cold, was slumped beside her.

Inspirationally, Bert leaped. He pulled open the Pontiac's door, shoved Jenny along the seat, and said, 'We've got to get Ernest out of here fast or he's a cooked goose. I've been looking for the kid all night.'

'In,' Jenny asked with the pent-up irritability of a hideous half dozen past hours, 'a pair of wet swim trunks?'

'Don't get smart,' Bert said viciously, and shot the Pontiac into reverse. Then he headed for the entrance and gave her the gun, with a lurch that almost caused him to sideswipe the Lincoln coupé of the Cardigan Bags, who were foggily rolling home after having put the Club Sans Souci to bed.

A word about the Cardigan Bags. They were twin sisters of uncertain age from Akron, Ohio, where their parents had died and left them in the unappetizing role of spinsterhood, but also heiresses to some tons of well-invested pelf derived from the manufacture of tires. Both being alcoholics in a nice, genteel way, they lived in a steamy haze of liquid fun, retaining just enough co-ordination to permit them to drive their car from oasis to oasis without committing suicide.

It explains why, when they talked with Duggan a few minutes after their brush with the Pontiac, their account of the incident had the dubious cohesion and vague edges of a tired blancmange.

It was, they told him in counterpoint, a miracle that they had escaped with their lives. Bert Jackson, who was driving and whom they recognized, had shot toward them like a madman, and with him, looking frightened, was Jenny Spang, and on her other side, looking dead, was Ernest Dean.

'Was this car,' Duggan asked a twin, 'a black convertible Cadillac with a lemon top?'

'We didn't notice,' the twin said.

'We didn't care,' the other twin said.

'We had no time for lemon tops.'

'And anyhow, whatever it was, it was down.'

'The top?' Duggan asked.

'It must have been, because the three of them were all sticking out in the open.'

'Like three leaves. That's the way they went by us. Like three flutted leaves in a great big terrible gale.'

This was good enough for Duggan, even the 'flutted,' whatever that stood for in the dictionary of dipsos. It was a wonder, what with the alcoholic scud through which at the moment they were enjoying life, that they had been able to differentiate between a convertible and an armored tank. It puzzled him briefly that the general alarm had not been effective and the Caddy picked up, but he put it down to the darkness and the fact that the emphasis of search had lain around Palm Beach and, presumably, to the north. Now that daylight was on hand, he felt satisfied that some cruiser would spot and stop the car.

But would Bert stop?

Duggan grew cold at the realization that of course Bert wouldn't. He felt reasonably certain that Bert wasn't armed, hadn't paused to gather up some weapon, but the car itself was a weapon with the deadly power of a fatal crash during a chase.

He hurried to the nearest telephone, which was in the manager's quarters, and worked himself into a sweat, emending the general alarm to the effect that the people in the black Cadillac convertible with the lemon top now numbered three, that the man at the wheel was a killer in the process both of escaping and of abducting the other two occupants. Extreme caution was to be exercised to prevent crash injuries during apprehension.

★   ★   ★

There was almost no traffic, and Bert made good time, crossing the Intracoastal Waterway's bridge at Dania, then charting his course toward the ultimate destination of a cypress swamp in Collier County as hard as he could shove it. He knew of a hunting shack in one of the savannas, having once visited it with Ernest and one of Ernest's native bar buddies. It was a dream spot for any angle you could think of. Plenty of sinkholes to swallow things up.

There was dough in Ernest, dead or alive. Contact the family lawyer — Bert had met him several times at the Deans' — and arrange a foolproof drop for the ransom. Then Mexico, Brazil, Timbuktu — who cares? And the girl. She could be used to keep Dean in line. Make a corkscrew out of her arms, and Dean would be begging him to accept the dough. A laugh.

Swamp country. Muck, and the fungus-like, rotting smell of water. They said the turkey buzzards pecked your eyes out first.

His stomach contracted into knots as he spotted a highway-patrol car up ahead, drawn up lazy on the shoulder at an intersection. He glanced at Jenny, pale and stringy and frightened, and his voice had the threat of a gun at her head.

'Quit figuring, sister. One move, one yelp out of you as we pass them, and you'll be deader than most. Just sit still and play it cool.'

He slowed circumspectly and sweated with relief when the patrol car's two uniformed occupants gave the Pontiac little more than a cursory glance. He figured how much time had passed. The Cardigan Bags had spotted his take-off and, even though they were constantly potted, he could tell they had recognized him. It was a cinch that Duggan would shoot out a general alarm.

Bert looked at the car's radio. It had no band for police calls, but the regular channels surely would be carrying an account of the choke job by now, maybe even on-the-spot-stuff from the motel. The Dean name was newsworthy enough for it.

He tuned in and caught the close of a Miami newscast:

' . . . barely missing a Lincoln coupé driven by Miss Evelyn Cardigan, who was returning from a night club with her twin sister, Miss Lily Cardigan. The sisters are from Akron, Ohio, and are the heiresses to Fleetwood Tires. Although slightly suffering from shock, they granted your reporter an interview, and here is a tape recording of their description of the getaway car:

''Did you get a good look at the occupants, Miss Cardigan?'

''Perfect. Positively perfect.'

''After all, they were almost dumped into our laps.'

''No, Lily, we were almost dumped into theirs.'

''Did you identify the make of the car?'

''Absolutely. We gave a detailed description of it to dear Chief Duggan.'

''What make was it, Miss Cardigan?'

''A Cadillac convertible. Black, and with a lemon top.'

''Did you get the license number, Miss Cardigan?'

''We didn't.'

''We felt too faint.'

'The Misses Cardigan again succumbed to shock at this point, and the interview closed. We will bring you constant bulletins throughout the morning as they come in, and now, after a brief pause, the weather.'

Bert clicked off the switch. He said, 'Brother, what a break! Those two dipsos are steamed up to the gills.'

'They always are,' Jenny said.

'Black Caddy! Lemon top! It's a wonder they didn't dream up six lizards in green pants.'

He was filled with a terrific exultation and an almost drunken sense of absolute security. He was getting the breaks and all he had to do was to roll with them to keep them coming his way. He felt good. Caesar good, all through. He wished he had a cigar.

'Bert — '

In this excess of warm comfortableness he said almost pleasantly, 'Well?'

'The unborn child — all the rest I could maybe understand — '

He snapped into ice.

'Cut the string section, sister. What about the kid? It was mine, wasn't it?'

A rush of wonder swept Jenny with the feel of mountain streams.

'Yours — and Miss Sangford's?'

'Miss Sangford in the pig's rear bumper. That tramp was Mrs. Bert Jackson before she took a nose dive into bigamy by becoming Mrs. Ernest Dean. Him — ' Bert cast a contemptuous look at Ernest. 'That night when we fixed it for her to hook him, Theda told me afterward that he wasn't even able to kick off his shoes.'

'Then there was no marriage, legally?'

Bert blazed impatiently, 'Why do you think I killed her? That nitwit brain of hers had it all figured down to a dime. First she figured I was holding out on the take, which I was. Then she figured on selling out. Big pay-off stuff, with me in the ashcan.'

'She'd admit to bigamy?'

'She could play it a number of ways, all of them to her very rosy. And there was nothing I could do. So I did it.' He looked at Jenny with flat, killer eyes. 'So be a good girl, Jenny, or I'll belt you out into left field.'

★ ★ ★

The sun rode higher, and County Attorney Oswald Pinker finished packing a bag for a short weekend jaunt to Nassau as a guest of the Tommy Andersons aboard their diesel yacht, *Carp II*.

Pinker was a magnetic, energetically agreeable man in his thirties, with a first-rate legal mind and a courtroom manner that could have given Miss Fernandez's repertoire of histrionics a point or two to think about. He was well regarded, both by the yacht-club set and by his party's political machine as a smooth, brilliant cookie who was destined to go far.

His home near the county seat, which he occupied with his wife Celeste and their three children, was a handsome ranch-style structure and one that could be easily expanded into a summer mansion appropriate for a governorship.

The telephone rang, and Pinker found Dr. Lawrence Ford, the county medical examiner, on the line.

'Thought you might want to know, Oz,' Ford said. 'Those two homicides in

Halcyon are turning into pretty hot stuff.'

'Homicides? Two? I thought it was a simple drowning.'

'That was what it looked like at first, but Sibley says it's definitely murder. With a repeat last night, presumably by the same joe, of a strangling.'

'Look — take it easy, Larry. I just got up. Been packing for Nassau with the Andersons.'

'Better unpack, Oz. This has busted out into main-line stuff — socialites, money, abduction, nationwide coverage. Sibley's given me a run-down for as far as he knows.'

Ford relayed as much of the situation as he had gathered from Sibley. Reluctantly Pinker canceled the Nassau cruise and headed his car for Halcyon.

He found the motel, already filled to mid-season capacity, further overrun with the press, the wire services, radio, and TV. He diplomatically ran this gantlet and finally was closeted alone with Duggan in the unit that had been occupied by Theda Sangford and in which Duggan had set up shop. Every other rental was splitting its seams.

They shook hands. Pinker wiped his brow. 'Let's get on,' he said. 'Right now the job reads like a page from *Through the Looking-Glass* — a floater that isn't, a matricide that isn't, an arrest that isn't, and some rigmarole about a Gettler test busting the case wide open. Just what is a Gettler test?'

'Basically it's used to prove drowning.'

'But we knew that. That the Sangford woman was drowned.'

'Sure, but we didn't know how. Or where.'

'Where? Sort of silly, isn't it? To section off the Atlantic Ocean — X marks the wave?'

Duggan smiled back. 'That isn't the angle. The real value of the Gettler test is that it can show whether the drowning took place in fresh water or in salt.'

Pinker was immediately interested. Here was something he could use, really sink his teeth into and dramatically present before a jury. Like the cornucopia trick with the colored silks.

'Tell me,' he said, 'exactly how.'

'Well, let's take the heart. There's two

of them, two sides really. The left and the right. When a guy drowns he inhales water, and this water is absorbed into the blood of the pulmonary veins and finally reaches the left heart.'

'I get the emphasis.'

'Now, if the drowning takes place in fresh water, the left heart's blood contains less sodium chloride than the right.'

'Sodium chloride, if I remember my primer, being plain, common salt.'

'Just about, but try and catch an M.D. admitting it. Then, on the other hand, if the drowning took place in sea water, the left heart would contain a much higher saline content than the right. That's what the Gettler test is based on.'

'I see where you're heading. But, look here, take that swimming pool out there. That's fresh water, certainly so far as a jury's notion of it is concerned, and yet it's purified by chlorination. The defense is bound to latch onto that angle and make a field day of it. Doesn't it throw the test out of the window?'

'No. By state specification the chlorine content of swimming pools must be kept down within minus point four and minus point six percent. Sibley adjusted for that in his analysis. Sangford was drowned in fresh water, but not in a fresh-water, chlorinated pool. She was drowned in that bathtub right inside that room there.'

'Apart from the Gettler test, got any evidence?'

'Plenty. The minute I saw the body I knew the setup was wrong. You see, I've been a lifeguard. I'm familiar with floaters. There was the way the body lay and the pattern of sand that had dried on her skin.'

'Sand patterns. Interesting. I'll use them. What was unique about them?'

Duggan, from papers on the desk, selected two photographs that Roth had taken. He handed them to Pinker.

'Take a look.'

Pinker studied the shots intently. 'I'd say she'd first been dumped down flat, then arranged on her side. If she'd been washed ashore she'd have been more bundled, and the tide would have cleaned off the sand.'

'That's exactly what's unique about the

patterns. There shouldn't be any. Then her hair. There was no bathing cap.'

'But don't they thrash around? Couldn't she have yanked it off herself while drowning? I'm simply exploring the defense again, Duggan. We know she never wore one. Not in a tub. What about the hair?'

'Some of it had streaked over her face and I brushed it back. Near the scalp it was not only damp but soft damp, fresh-water damp, not sticky.'

'That's a pretty fine distinction, isn't it?'

'Very. Not a guy in a hundred would notice it, and it will get you nowhere as evidence. But there was hair oil, and that will.'

'Yes, it's good — salt water would wash the oil off with any sort of submersion, but not a short ducking under fresh.'

'Then there are the bruise marks on her ankles, when he yanked her up by the feet to pull her head under.'

'Do you know something? It's like that famous old case in England when bathtubs were still a novelty. Was it England or here?'

'I remember the one you mean. The guy married a bunch of wives, caught their heels while they took a bath, yanked up, and their heads went under. And right away he was once more a rich widower. Simple as pie. Only Jackson elaborated. He dumped the body by the sea before proposed Suspect Number One, young Dean, was due to trot down to the beach for a daybreak rendezvous.'

'Slow up a bit. I'm puzzled about how come Miss Sangford would lie quietly, and I might add fully exposed, in a tub of water and let Jackson wander in without her yelping?'

'No trouble there. They were married. About a year before she bought herself a bigamy charge by marrying Dean. I got that from New York when they put Sangford's record through the mill.'

'Then that's the motive — bigamy. That kid she was going to have figures too, wouldn't you say?'

'Sure to be along those lines. I think she was dealing Jackson out. We'll dig it out of him. Incidentally, she took that bath about four in the morning, probably to try and sober her wits before Jackson got there. We can be pretty certain she was expecting him.'

'How?'

'She had Jimmy, the bartender, drop off a couple of bottles of scotch after the bar closed. Jackson's fingerprints are on one of them. Probably needed a slug after he'd finished the tub end of the job.'

Pinker was enchanted. 'That nails it. That nails him smack on the scene of the crime. Wonder why he was careless? Didn't wipe off things in here he'd touched?'

'He was conceited enough to be positive this would never be considered the scene of the killing. He'd have made book that the ocean would be officially accepted as the spot, with young Dean set up alongside as the prize goat.'

Pinker mulled for a moment such evidence as there was at hand, digesting it, dovetailing it with the more general picture he had been given earlier over the telephone by the medical examiner.

'Tell me,' he said, 'what put you onto him? Almost everything pointed toward Dean, or his mother, or even the Spangs.'

'His lies, and the fact that he held the key position in the whole setup.'

'Amazing, isn't it, how even the smartest of them will lie and expect to get away with it?'

'They get cocky. Jackson knew we had no reason to suspect him — that's while I first was questioning him about the Sangford-Dean marriage deal — and that's when he slipped.'

'What did he lie about?'

'Telling about the couple of months during which he acted as pay-off man for Dean to keep the marriage under the hatch. Jackson claimed he knew nothing about Sangford whatever, didn't know where she lived, said she always contacted him by phone at the Deans' and arranged a time and meeting place. Well, in the first place it seemed funny to me that he hadn't tailed her; then when her record came through from New York, listing her as a probable call girl from a small book of men's numbers by the phone in her apartment — '

'Of course. You checked the telephone directory.'

'Our local operator had a Manhattan book and she looked it up. Theda Sangford was listed in it for anybody to see, and that laid Jackson's story about not knowing where she lived wide open. The rest was simple arithmetic.'

'What a complete louse. Think of it, Duggan. His own wife for bait. Now about the strangling — I suppose Mrs. Dean got onto something, or else Jackson thought she had.'

'He knew she was waiting, and her patience was out of character.' Duggan became succinct. He was increasingly worried as to why the general alarm for the Cadillac didn't show results. He said tersely, 'Jackson knew that a woman like Mrs. Dean would have blasted him the minute she found out he had two-timed her about the secret marriage. Unless she was getting wise to a hotter vengeance — like his being the killer. Actually, Mrs. Spang was told by Mrs. Dean that Mrs. Dean 'knew something.' The word spread, and naturally Jackson got it. To him, it fitted. Same setup with Fernandez.'

'You planted that, of course.'

'Sure, and those things will be confirmed when we nab him — along with odds and ends like a funnel, rubber gloves, how he missed finding the Dean marriage certificate, and et cetera. But right now I'm worried — bad.'

'About Dean and Miss Spang? So am I. I suppose the only reason why they haven't been spotted is that they've holed in.'

'No, I've been thinking. There may be another answer. Mario.' Duggan put through a call for the Club Continental, and a harsh male voice barked, 'Yes?'

'I'm Duggan. Police Chief, Halcyon. I want to speak with Mario.'

'You can't. He's asleep. He never gets up before three in the afternoon.'

'Wake him.'

'Are you kidding?'

'You heard me.'

'It's a tough job, Chief.'

'Do it.'

'Well, if you say so.'

Shortly Mario's rich voice said frowsily, 'It is I, Mario. Why do you do this bad thing to me, Duggan?'

'Why did you lie to me?'

Mario's voice was complacent. 'Ah — my little fib.'

'Your little fib may result in killing Dean and Miss Spang.'

'Do not joke with me while I am sleeping.'

'Get this, Mario. Dean and Jenny Spang have been kidnapped by Jackson.'

'That is so terrible? A watchdog gathers up his sheep? For that I am woke up at' — Mario's voice plunged into horror — 'mama mia, it is but eleven o'clock!'

'For God's sake, snap out of it. Jackson's no watchdog. He's a killer. He's the killer. Does that sink in?'

Mario's voice sharped to complete seriousness. 'Yes, and at once I will tell you. If anything should happen to those two nice rich kids because of me I would kill myself.'

'That, I doubt.'

'No matter. It is a noble thought. When Mr. Dean comes to my office last night he cashes this check for one thousand dollars. But it is not for the cages or the wheel. He has arranged a plan during the daytime in secret with Miss Spang. They are to elope. They are to drive to Georgia, where you can get married simply by opening your mouth — Duggan, why are they not now in Georgia?'

'I don't know. Get back on line.'

'It is true as I told you last night that I loaned him a car, but it was not one of the Cadillacs.'

'Why did you say that it was?'

'I didn't. You did. It was a thing you took for granted. Me, I simply played along. Remember?'

Duggan remembered. 'But why?' he asked.

'So that Mr. Dean would not be disturbed on his honeymoon. It would have been indelicate to let him be hauled back by cops for the foolish reason that his mother got herself justifiably killed. I am a sentimental man.'

'Mr. Shylock was too. What car did Dean take?'

'I told Slick to give him any car he wanted, and he took Slick's.'

'What make?'

'It is a Pontiac convertible. Very red all

over, which may be why it appealed to Mr. Dean for the happy occasion. Most festive.'

'Don't crowd it. What year? License number?'

'You will relax while I find out such things from Slick. He is by my side. It is he who risked his life to wake me up.'

After a muttered off-the-line conversation, Mario's voice returned and gave Duggan the data he wanted. Duggan thanked him, jotted the license number of the Pontiac on a pad, and hung up.

'Wrong car?' Pinker asked.

'Wrong car.'

★ ★ ★

The canal alongside the road was choked with suede green leaves and the lavender of water hyacinth, while high in the shimmery heat over sage palmetto fans and turpentine trees a buzzard lazed.

For mile after safe, swift mile Bert, like spring, had been busting out all over with an almost drunken, arrogant sense of content. Boy, he told himself happily, you've got a rainbow round your shoulder. Along this sparsely traveled stretch, which led to the cutoff through the savanna to the hunting shack, nothing could happen, and the dangerous part of the job would be over. The initial flight.

Even along the more populated highways the luck had held. One road-patrol car, one cruiser from the sheriff's office. A steady forty-per in passing them and all had been smooth. One thought had bothered: his being in swim trunks. But he was also, he remembered, in Florida, where plenty of joes you saw in cars looked stripped.

And here along this desolate route he was satisfied, from frequent glancings in the rear-view mirror, that he had no tail. Only that buzzard hanging in the sky. Only that yellow helicopter traipsing away like an old maid in long skirts far up above in the hot, cloudless blue. From, Bert casually thought, one of the fields in the general area.

A sputter brought his eyes sharply to the panel. The gas indicator stood at Empty. A towering rage swept over him at his own lulled stupidity.

'When did you fill this crate last?' he snapped at Jenny.

'We were going to last night, but we stopped at a roadhouse and Ernest — well, when we came out Ernest couldn't drive.'

'I've been wondering why you turned back.'

'I couldn't face it. Landing at that hour of the night someplace with Ernest the way he was and — '

'Skip the blueprints.' Bert threw a disgusted look at the wreck on her other side. 'How a neat package like you could ever tie up with a ribbon-winner stewpot like him. It gets me.'

'I love him. I love him very much.'

Bert reserved his blistering reaction to this starched lace valentine as his rage vanished before visual proof that his luck was still hot. A piece ahead, just coming into eye reach like a blessing, stood what resembled a small, weather-tired general store. Two gas pumps were before its porch.

Bert coasted onto the shoulder, the car's engine dead. He indulged in swift reflection. The distant store looked lifeless and the car, he felt, would still have been unobserved.

'Stay put,' he said to Jenny.

He got out and opened the luggage compartment. Among its small litter of contents a length of towline and a wipe rag pleased him.

He said to Jenny, 'Get out.'

'What are you going to do?'

Bert leaned loosely on the open door.

'Do you play it my way, or do you get a tire iron shacked up in your head?'

Jenny got out. Using the towline and the wipe rag, he wrapped her up. He lifted her into the luggage compartment and slammed the lid. He fished the wallet from Ernest's pocket and was enchanted to find that it held, at a rough estimate, over eight or nine hundred bucks. Carrying it in his hand, he walked toward the store.

It was farther away than it had seemed, and his bare feet burned with every step as they flattened on the blacktop. This, however, was a minor irritation. The over-all picture continued sound. He got to the store and hoped that somebody inside its dying shell would still be alive. He went into a twilight clutter.

'Anybody here?' he called.

A door opened in the room's rear and a bovine young woman, bulging in a play suit, came out of the shadows and inspected him.

'Been swimming, mister?'

'Many times, sugar ball, and let's cut the Abbott-and-Costello, shall we? I'm out of gas. Got a gallon can? I'll fill up when I bring it back.'

'I'll go look and see. I think Ezra left an empty in the utility room maybe a week or so ago.'

Minutes treacled through Bert's impatience in the fly-buzzing shade, and mosquitoes, abroad from the surrounding swampland, pulled their sneak attacks. Finally, after a good endless quarter of an hour, the young woman returned.

'I got a can.'

He said irritably, 'That's peachy, ma'am. Just peachy. Let's fill it.'

The can was filled. He gave her a five-dollar bill.

'Hold it,' he said, 'until I come back.'

He set off toward the car and looked ahead, and his stomach was gripped by inside hands that almost twisted his guts out as he saw that a patrol car was parked alongside the Pontiac. His luck blew up in his head. He dropped the can of gas and tensed to make an offside sprint into the palmettos.

'Don't try it, Jackson,' a voice behind him said.

The sheriff's deputy was not only a big young man but his right hand held what looked to Bert like a cannon.

'Just keep moving along the road,' the deputy said.

Bert moved. He clutched after shredded lifebelts.

'You've got no call to jump me like this.'

The deputy's voice was hard and exact. 'You are under arrest for abduction and murder.'

'You've got the wrong car. I heard the alarm. Black Caddy with a lemon top. Does that bus of mine — '

'Save it. You heard the call Duggan had them keep sending out on the regular broadcast channels. The general he put through on the police bands called for a red Pontiac convertible, which is just what you've got. That firecracker blazed a trail two yards wide, and we were just laying off until you stopped.'

'I kept looking back — '

'Sure you did. So did that helicopter up there. Two-way radio communication, Jackson. Field glasses. They even spotted your storage job of the girl in the trunk.'

★ ★ ★

The midday siesta-hour sun blazed down on Black's, and Miss Fernandez applied another pat of eau de cologne to Mrs. Spang's fevered brow. If only, if only, Mrs. Spang begged in silent prayer, they would come back alive. Then everything, the whole great big beautiful world, would be peaches and cream.

She already had the major outlines for the wedding planned. St. Thomas's, of course, with a reception in the Waldorf-Astoria.

Naturally there must be a wait, a decent

interval between Mrs. Dean's shocking death and the divine event, but the time would not be wasted. During it Mrs. Spang planned to embrace dear Ernest within the same wise, gentle coils with which she had hog-tied dear Jenny. Yes, generously, self-sacrificially, she would assume the tender leadership once held by the dear boy's dead mother. Always having his best interests at heart. And his dough.

'You are being awfully good to me,' she said to Miss Fernandez. 'To stand by like this during these terrible hours of anxiety.'

'We are all children of God, madame. Even the bad ones of us.'

'You can't mean that literally. Not Bert Jackson.'

'Even he.'

Mrs. Spang was saved from replying to this outrageous nonsense by Duggan, who came in and said, 'It's all right. I've just had word. The sheriff's patrol is bringing them in. All safe. All done.'

Later, in a charming restaurant back of Halcyon, away from people and places where they would be recognized, Miss Fernandez entertained Mrs. Spang and her daughter and a revived Ernest at dinner.

It was a pleasant meal, candle-lit, and served on a screened veranda overlooking a garden lush with flora of the semi-tropics. One incident would always remain, Miss Fernandez knew, happy in her thoughts.

Mrs. Spang, during the baked pompano, said incisively to Ernest, 'I have decided that about two months would be proper.'

'For what, Mrs. Spang?'

'To show respect for your dear mother. An elaborate wedding before then would be in bad taste. After the ceremony, I thought we could take an extended tour. Possibly Brazil and the Argentine. You are not to worry about a thing, dear Ernest.'

Ernest looked at her thoughtfully.

'I'm not, Mrs. Spang.'

'As long as there is a breath left in me I shall try to make up for your loss.'

'We appreciate that, Mrs. Spang. Both Jenny and I. But I'm afraid there won't be too many opportunities.'

A chilly hand seemed to stroke Mrs. Spang's aging spine.

'Opportunities? I simply don't under-stand?'

'We will wait until the inquest and the funeral are over, Jenny and I. Then we think a quiet church wedding, after which we're motoring West until the trial comes. We'll be planning where we care to live. Jenny and I, Mrs. Spang. Naturally we will arrange to have you settled wherever you may wish.'

Miss Fernandez signaled their waiter to pour more champagne.

'I shall advance a toast.' She raised her glass. She looked at Ernest with fond, relieved eyes and said, 'Good friend — to your coming of age.'

Malice in Wonderland

When Alice Wickershield was a little girl of nine and still believed in all the childhood wonderlands with their fantasy inhabitants, she was given a birthday party by an old woman whom she firmly considered to be a witch.

Alice frequently remarked to her best friend, Elsie Grunwald, 'The tip of Mrs. Fleury's nose almost touches her chin, and that is a sign.'

Elsie, who was of a similar age but completely disillusioned as to the fey, would answer practically, 'That is because she hates wearing false teeth.'

There the matter would drop until some later event would again bring Mrs. Fleury under scrutiny. Naturally, Mrs. Fleury being the hostess, the birthday party brought the subject of her cabalistic specialty into focus once more.

Alice lived with her father (her mother was dead) in a house of Early Boom design in the town of Halcyon, on the Florida coast to the north of Miami. Their neighbors on the west were the Grunwalds, whose only child Elsie was Alice's best friend; and on the other side was the sorceress with her old-fashioned, galleried home appropriately shrouded in dank grounds of somber tropical plantings.

The birthday party was in late June and, as school was over for the season, the festivities were able to get under way shortly after the noon hour with a series of mildly competitive games under the palm and ficus trees that smothered the grounds with their shade. It was at the conclusion of the games and the distribution of prizes, with each of the children miraculously having won one, that luncheon was served in the patio, and Mrs. Fleury's witchery meshed into gear and determined, eleven years later, the question of Alice's fate.

Dessert for the luncheon was a delicious treat put up especially for Mrs. Fleury by a local company. It consisted of ice cream tropical fish of various flavors and colors, with each mold resting artistically on a foamy wave of spun sugar. At the side of each plate with its chill confection was a cracker bonbon, or snapper, that went bang when its ends were sharply pulled, and hid a strip of paper on which was printed a motto that was presumed to shed a prophetic light on the puller's future.

'Children,' Mrs. Fleury said, 'I am going to command a test for your powers of self-control — Jefferson Hollingsworth, put down that cracker bonbon until you hear what I have to say.'

'This is it,' whispered Alice to Elsie. 'Look at her chin.'

Mrs. Fleury waited until Jefferson Hollingsworth, a handsome youngster with liquid, chestnut eyes, reluctantly replaced his snapper beside a frozen version of a pistachio-and-raspberry carp.

'I am going to ask that each little guest take his or her cracker bonbon home and that you do not tear it open until some moment of the most desperate nature may come to you during your lifetimes. As you know, the crackers conceal a printed motto, and it is my wish for you

— and for Alice in particular because it is her birthday anniversary — that the message conveyed in the motto shall guide you during this future crisis of either joy or sorrow to do the right, the happy thing.'

'She is asking one hell of a lot from kids,' Harold Grunwald said to his wife Sidonia after Elsie had returned from the party and reported the odd incident. 'I'd say the old bat has lost her marbles.'

'Well' — Sidonia laughed — 'it was too much for Elsie, and where that child gets her I.Q. from I wouldn't know. She produced a logical enough crisis out of a hat.'

'She gets her I.Q. from me. At her age I had mastered the Morse code in preparation for becoming an international spy, and last month I merely mentioned the fact and Elsie picked out Mata Hari as her dream career in womanhood and can already send six words a minute in Morse. She uses her pal Alice as a receiving set.'

'So that's why they've been tapping on things and looking remote.'

'It is. And what's this about a logical crisis?'

'Simply that Elsie opened her cracker bonbon before she even set foot here in the house. She claimed the rich food at the party made her feel critically bilious, so she ripped out the motto.'

'And what was the prophetic suggestion? Citrate of magnesia?'

'No, it was a rather horrid quotation from Shakespeare: Open, locks, Whoever knocks!'

'What's so horrible in that?'

Sidonia, who was tons more intellectual than her husband (she had majored in English at Barry College), said, 'It doesn't give the entire quotation. It's simply taken out of context.'

'Put it back in again.'

'It goes, By the pricking of my thumbs, something wicked this way comes. Open, locks, Whoever knocks!'

Mr. Grunwald, becoming bored with the matter and wanting to get on with the do-it-yourself parakeet cage he was making, said, 'All that superstitious rubbish is silly.'

'I don't know. I honestly don't know,

Hal. Sometimes I wonder.'

Two weeks later Elsie, while presumably stitching up a ball costume for her favorite doll in the seclusion of the Grunwalds' allamanda-draped gazebo, totally disappeared.

★　★　★

With the exception of Alice, all the children had followed Elsie's impulse and torn open their favors. They had read the time-weary little mottoes, been momentarily captivated by the tissue-paper hats, the modest souvenirs, and then had thrown the whole works into a wastebasket and out of their minds.

Not Alice.

Because she still believed in the wondrous, Alice had put her cracker bonbon in her treasure chest — a cardboard shoe box fancifully pasted over with Christmas wrappings — along with her diary, a dried toadstool highly favored as a parasol by elves, and sundry other articles of enduring sentiment.

It was only natural that, being Elsie's

most intimate companion, Alice should have been questioned more patiently and closely than any of the other children after Elsie had 'gone away' — that phrase being considered by their elders as most suitable to cover the desperately serious reality. Alice bore the questioning stoically and only broke down once, when she asked Mrs. Grunwald whether she might keep the doll's ball gown that Elsie had been sewing on in the gazebo to remember Elsie by.

'But Elsie is coming back, dear,' Sidonia said, restraining by the greatest will power her own tears of torture and doubt.

'No, she isn't, Mrs. Grunwald. She was put under a spell by Mrs. Fleury, and that's the end of her.'

'A spell, Alice?' Sidonia repeated as her eyes narrowed speculatively, as though herein might lie some clue, however preposterous, to the fate of her lost child. 'What do you mean by a spell, dear?'

'Mrs. Fleury is a witch, and Elsie disobeyed her express command by opening her cracker bonbon on such a silly excuse.

A stomach-ache is not a crisis.'

Alice left the interview, taking with her the doll's unfinished ball gown, with its needle and length of unused thread still stuck in lemonade-colored satin. She wrapped the dress around her own cracker bonbon, as both seemed to be linked in their special magical field, and returned them to the treasure chest where they were to lie fallow in their diablerie for many years to come.

When Hal Grunwald came home that night after a harrowing day spent with the police, the sheriff's deputies, and the road patrols, all of whom were searching for Elsie during this second day of her disappearance, Sidonia told him what Alice had said about Mrs. Fleury being a witch, and he hit the ceiling.

He then collapsed dog-tired into a chair and held his hot head in his hands and said, 'Oh my God, Sid, you could listen to childish drivel while we're moving heaven and earth to find her.'

'I'd listen to any sort of drivel if I thought it would do any good. After all, Hal, what do we know about Mrs. Fleury?'

146

'We know what she has told us.'

'That's exactly what I mean about our life here. The friends we make come from all over the country and we don't know a thing about them except what they tell us themselves.'

Sidonia, who had been holding her control by superhuman effort during the past two tragic days and nights, grew hysterical and her voice broke in odd high notes.

'We exercise more judgment about our servants than we do about our friends,' she went on with those shrillish overtones. 'We check servants, look up references — why, they even have police cards of identity. But our friends? We let our children associate with them and we don't know what they are. Mrs. Fleury? From Cleveland, she says, widowed — her husband left her well off — and we smile and swallow it. She might be a mass poisoner for all we know. Alice claims she's a witch, and you laugh. Well, a child's judgment might be better than our judgment. A child's eyes see things clearly, not through a fog of polite social conventions.'

'Sid, knock it off, will you? We're both carrying all the traffic will bear without getting sidetracked into black magic.'

The ransom note came that night.

With the vivid imagination of childhood Alice arranged all the fragments of overheard talks between her father and his friends into a factual whole. A ransom had been demanded, fifty thousand dollars had been paid, and Elsie still had not returned home.

'She can't,' Alice said to Sidonia when they met by chance at the hibiscus border that divided the Wickershield and Grunwald properties. 'She can't come back because she's dead.'

'Darling, don't say it. Oh, don't even think it.' Sidonia plunged through the hedge and, getting down on her knees, gripped Alice's hands so hard that the bones felt all together. 'You must tell me — I am begging this of you, Alice — isn't there something you know? Something real?'

'Witches are real.'

Sidonia looked at the child searchingly, half convinced in the torture-ridden

148

uncertainties of her cracking mind that the fateful motto just might have had something to do with their loss.

'You really believe that, Alice, don't you?'

'It's dangerous not to.'

'Then destroy it. Burn your cracker bonbon. Get it now and burn it up.'

'I can't.'

'Why not?'

'Because it isn't time.'

So intense is the power of public opinion that Mrs. Fleury began feeling it on all sides — to the extent that she concluded the only answer lay in selling her place and leaving Halcyon.

The children beleaguered her from a safe distance with cries of witch-witch-witch, and the elders forming her circle of friends were electrically artificial in their greetings and perfunctory smiles.

Even the police thoroughly checked her whereabouts during the hour when Elsie had been sewing by herself in the gazebo. They handled the inquiry discreetly, of course, and no mention was made of it officially, but the fact was shortly general knowledge that Mrs. Fleury had an ironclad alibi. She had been undergoing the rack of a hair and facial treatment at the shop of Halcyon's best and most talkative beautician.

In Alice's opinion this absolute alibi was futile for a witch, they being a breed notoriously famous for their astral ability to be in two different places at the same time, and she announced as much to the other children, who promptly stepped up their campaign of torment instead of dropping it.

Mrs. Fleury was unable to fight back, any more than she could have fought the invisible vapors from a swamp with her bare fists. Fortunately she found a ready buyer for her home in Dr. Jessup Hollingsworth, whose adopted son Jefferson had had to be cautioned at the birthday party against a premature snapping of his cracker bonbon.

Since coming to Halcyon over a year ago, Dr. Hollingsworth had been living with Jeff in the sterile splendor of a beach hotel.

The doctor had reached the age of

retirement and wanted to settle down.

'I want roots,' he said to Haidee Glosser in her real estate office in town. 'Not so much for myself as for Jefferson. My wife's tragic death made it impossible to continue living in our former home in New York.'

'I understand,' Miss Glosser murmured with sympathy while mentally pocketing a fat commission for the Fleury estate.

Within less than a week the deal was closed. Mrs. Fleury moved to the west coast and settled in St. Petersburg, which was, so far as east coast Floridians were concerned, as far away as Siberia. And Alice acquired a new best friend.

She and young Jeff Hollingsworth were classmates in elementary school, it was true, but there had been none of the special affinity that goes with a friendship on a next-door basis once the initial ice of propinquity is melted — and at the age of nine the thaw comes fast.

'How do you like being adopted?' Alice asked during the preliminaries.

'There's not much feeling about it,' Jeff said.

'What happened to your adopted mother?'

'Foster mother.'

'Foster. Thank you.'

'Don't mention it. She was killed by a hit-and-run driver right after my adoption papers went through. I only remember her looks.'

'What did she look like?'

'Like anybody.'

'What are you going to be, Jeff, when you grow up?'

'A botanist.'

'Why?'

'Because plants and trees and flowers are important. They can be like people, only nicer. I've got leaves and specimens of about almost everything around here. Each one is dried and labeled from where I found it.'

'Have you ever met any elves while you were gathering them?'

'No.'

'Do you believe in them, Jeff?'

'Maybe.'

★　★　★

Inevitably, as the years of childhood and the ensuing teens dreamed by, Alice and Jeff drew more seriously toward each other in their affections, and only Sidonia Grunwald, of the people who knew them, tried to put a damper on the intimacy.

Sidonia had never given up, nor would she, no matter how earnestly Hal begged her to resign herself to the inevitable. Elsie was gone but they, he said, were left and had their lives together to be lived.

'She isn't gone,' Sidonia would say with a kind of fierceness. 'She's someplace.'

Yes, Hal would think in his own emptiness, Elsie was someplace all right, and a stomach-wrenching vision would come to him of their darling's small bones lying unshriven in some secret desolation of the Everglades or under the water of rockpits or of hyacinth-smothered canals, year after lonely year in their whitening.

'I can't get it out of my head,' Sidonia would say wildly, 'that that place, that that woman had something to do with it.'

'I wish you'd stop poking around over there. I know you do at night, and apart from the fact that I'm sure it annoys Dr.

Hollingsworth, it just isn't healthy, Sid.'

'You can't be healthy with an empty heart.'

This fixed idea formed the basis for Sidonia's corroding reaction to the romance between young Jeff and Alice, whom she feverishly loved because there seemed to cling to the girl a lingering association with her lost Elsie. Actually, Sidonia was a little deranged on the subject, feeling herself constantly drawn to the old Fleury grounds (she never thought of it as the Hollingsworth place), and it was true, as Hal said, that she would steal over there and search around beneath its dank canopies, especially when the moon was full.

She had convinced herself of the half-demented syllogism that the grounds were under a curse, therefore Jeff and his foster father, since they lived within the influence of the grounds' baleful star, were also accursed. Sidonia wanted no part of this disastrous magic to rub off on Alice, not even through the medium of young love.

The college years brought no hiatus in the serious intentions between Alice and Jeff. She went to Barry in Miami Shores, and he attended the University of Miami in nearby Coral Gables. There Jeff delved deeply into the structure, physiology, and distribution of the members of the vegetable kingdom, with an ultimate aim of specializing in plant morphology. With this broadened knowledge Jeff, among later interests, had carefully emended his boyhood collection of specimens, which were still methodically kept on file in a small laboratory he had equipped at home.

Rather because she wanted to be near him than from any curiosity about botany, Alice would often stay with Jeff in the laboratory while he worked, and one day when he was reclassifying some specimens of his childhood collection her interest was caught by a closely set cluster of fine, slender branches.

'It looks like a little broom, Jeff.'

'It should. It's hexenbesen, more commonly known as witches'-broom.'

The name aroused stirrings of many years ago.

'Did you find it here? When Mrs. Fleury owned the place?'

'Not actually.'

He had picked it up, Jeff told her, from his foster father's bedroom floor in the beach hotel they had been staying at. He imagined it must have fallen from a cuff of Dr. Hollingsworth's trousers when he had taken them off the night before.

'I remember asking him about it. It's an unusual find, and I wanted to trace its source. It's an outgrowth caused by a plant parasite or fungus.'

'Did you?'

'Did I what?'

'Trace its source?'

'Not until after we'd moved here.'

Dr. Hollingsworth had told Jeff, when questioned, that he probably picked it up while looking over the grounds with the real estate agent just before purchasing them.

'I finally located it,' Jeff said, 'after we had moved in and I'd remembered that witches'-brooms sometimes appear on ferns — low enough to be caught in a cuff.'

'So it did come from here. Funny.'

'Why funny?'

'Don't you remember our thinking old Mrs. Fleury was a witch? At least I certainly did.'

'All kids think crazy stuff.'

'I know it and I realize now what a little fool I was about it. I'd like to see Mrs. Fleury again and tell her I'm sorry for having caused her to be pestered, for making her give up her home, really. Jeff — I wonder if she's still alive.'

'What makes you say that?'

'Just a feeling. A funny feeling, Jeff.'

They were to be married shortly after graduation, and Mr. Wickershield, Alice's father, finally persuaded Sidonia (in her self-assumed role of proxy mother to Alice) to handle all the intricate arrangements for the wedding.

'I still feel,' Sidonia said to Hal after she had reluctantly given way to Mr. Wickershield's urging, 'that the marriage would be a mistake. It's — it's sinister. Malign.'

'Oh please, Sid!'

Hal had grown stout and comfortable, and instead of continuing to be sympathetic he was getting irritated with what he thought of as Sidonia's perpetual mania and her occasional Ophelia-like nocturnal driftings around the old Fleury grounds. He had loved their lost Elsie with all his heart and he still loved her memory, but grief cannot live forever. If it did, he thought philosophically, all life on earth would die.

Dr. Hollingsworth, in his role of foster father, arranged the bachelor dinner for Jeff at a beach club of correct distinction — the groom's gift for the best man and the ushers being platinum cuff links from Tiffany, the food and wines compatible — and Jeff, whose familiarity with champagne was on only a nodding basis, got socked straight into left field. Unfortunately he remained on his feet, his talk intelligible, and his good night to the doorman who brought his car sounded (as the doorman later testified) all right. Otherwise, a taxi or a lift would have been firmly suggested.

A milkman, making his delivery shortly after sunup to the rear of Dr. Hollingsworth's house, found Sidonia crumpled under the hibiscus that edged the driveway to the garage. He was not a man to panic, thanks to Korea, and having determined that she was still alive, he roused the household. All, that is, but Jeff, who was still sprawled, fully dressed, across his bed in stuporous sleep.

★ ★ ★

. . . In the news of local interest (a Fort Lauderdale newscaster announced) the Halcyon police report an alleged drunk-driving accident on the grounds of Dr. Jessup Hollingsworth, formerly the old Fleury estate. The victim is a Mrs. Grunwald, a neighbor whose daughter Elsie was kidnapped a decade ago and presumably killed by her abductor after a ransom of fifty thousand dollars had been paid. The old kidnapping case remains unsolved. According to her husband and her close friends, this tragedy continued to prey on Mrs. Grunwald and caused her to take walks at night around the Hollingsworth grounds, which, they say, she associated in some fashion with her child's disappearance. The police theorize that she was on such an excursion last night when Dr. Hollingsworth's adopted son Jefferson drove home from a bachelor dinner in a drunken condition and struck Mrs. Grunwald. James

Cray, 2714 Northeast Hempstead Court, who delivers the morning milk, found her lying under an hibiscus hedge where she had been flung by the impact. She is now at Memorial, and her condition is pronounced critical . . .

* * *

The world came to an end, but Alice did not break down. With Jeff released under a five-thousand-dollar bail bond, with Sidonia's life suspended by a thread above the valley of death, Alice would make Jeff sit out the foreboding hours with her in the privacy of the Grunwalds' allamanda-draped gazebo, where they were reasonably sheltered from the press and even from their friends. When evening fell, each would go home to face the night with such courage as could be summoned.

'I don't suppose,' Alice's father said to her, cupping the mouthpiece of a telephone, on the second night following the accident, 'that you would care to talk with her? She's peculiarly persistent.'

'Who, Papa?'

'That woman who used to live next to us. You remember, a Mrs. Fleury. She's calling from St. Petersburg.'

Almost as though some extrasensory impulse were forcing her steps, Alice moved toward the phone.

'Alice, dear child,' Mrs. Fleury's (again) familiar voice came from the receiver, 'I have been reading all about it, and you will think me a silly old woman, but I felt compelled to telephone. I want to ask you just one question.'

'Yes, Mrs. Fleury?'

'Call me a superstitious old fool if you wish — I remember how you were childishly positive I was a witch' — Mrs. Fleury paused to give a forgiving, paperish little laugh — 'and perhaps I am one, because while I was reading about your fiancé's critical predicament, the most singular, almost clairvoyant vision popped into my mind. It made me feel exactly like one of the weird sisters, and I simply leaped on my witch's broom and flew to call you up. Now, tell me, Alice, do you remember the birthday party?'

'Of course, Mrs. Fleury.'

'Do you recall the cracker bonbons and my nonsensically mysterious instructions about them?'

'Yes.'

'Well, do you by the wildest chance still have yours?'

'Yes.'

'Is it still unopened?'

'Yes.'

'Then open it now.'

And the wire went dead.

★   ★   ★

Alice left her father still standing near the telephone, with Mr. Wickershield silently wondering just what the call had been all about in order to have affected his daughter in such an odd manner.

'I swear to you, Hal,' he told Harold Grunwald afterward, 'she positively drifted from the room as if she'd been put under a spell . . . '

The cardboard treasure chest, with its Christmas wrappings of holly, gold, and stars, had for years been lying undisturbed in the bottom drawer of a dresser in Alice's room.

Alice got it out and put it on a desk where the shaft from a metal cone-shaded lamp made startling the colors' holiday brilliance. With a reluctance that combined the fear ever present when brushing the unnatural and with a hope that she did not dare feel too strongly because of the impossible qualities that surrounded it, she took out the cracker bonbon in its covering of the doll's ball gown and pushed the treasure chest aside.

Then in her sudden eagerness Alice felt a finger pricked by the needle which was still caught in what had been Elsie's last stitch, and a drop of blood stained a pea-sized circle of red on the lemonade-colored satin of the little dress. Alice removed the dress and with no further ado took both ends of the cracker bonbon and pulled them sharply apart. The report, to her now more adult ears, produced but a trivial effect.

With a scissors she slit the white paper cover and, discarding a gay red paper hat and a miniature metal fire engine, she came at last to the strip of paper on which the motto was printed. An ugly wave of disappointment engulfed Alice as she read it. She had been expecting something truly prophetic — like Elsie's open, locks, Whoever knocks! which, she later had learned, had been out of its dire context.

The motto dropped from her fingers and came to rest on the ball gown beside the needle. She had hoped so much, Alice now admitted to herself — she had been hoping all along with her desperate heart for some sign — and now all her hopes had come to this childlike ending of — of —

Her eyes darted from the motto to the blood drop, to the needle, to the line of stitches, in the last one of which the needle had been left. Clear under the cone-shafted light they were visible in their good, straight line. There was only one thing the matter with it, Alice decided critically. The line ran diagonally across the front panel of the gown and therefore, from a dressmaker's point of view, not only served no purpose but was the act of a seamstress gone suddenly mad.

Never would Elsie, as Alice remembered her lost, best friend, with her fine capabilities in so many of the childhood arts, have been guilty of such botchery. Unless it were purposely done. And rarely had anything ever been done by Elsie that had lacked purpose.

Alice's pulse quickened as a ripple of strange excitement caught her brain, and she examined more closely the misplaced line of stitching. Not only was the line misplaced, but the stitches themselves were uneven in their spacing — another unthinkable thing for Elsie to have done.

Unless, again, it was purposely done.

So steeped was Alice in the flood made by the years rolled back that Elsie became real — with their best-friends tie and all their secrets of shattering importance and their fearless preparations for facing the entrancing vistas of adult life to come. Yes, Alice remembered, their last projected career had been to become Mata Hari, with all her fascinating background of international intrigue.

And for which they had both learned the Morse code.

Her eyes flew to the line of unevenly spaced stitches. Dots and dashes, sewn in chartreuse thread on lemonade-colored satin. The pencil in her fingers automatically put the letters down on the spread-open white paper wrapper of the cracker bonbon. DRHOLCRZYHLPM — then nothing more.

So intense, so feverish was Alice's excitement that little meant anything to her but that here was Elsie's last message on earth, and that within it undoubtedly lay a clue to her disappearance and, according to Mrs. Fleury, an agency of help in Jeff's and Alice's present deadly crisis.

Taking the ball gown with her and leaving the rest of the magical properties on the desk, with her heart going suffocatingly in hopeful thumps, Alice ran from her room and out of the house with no thought in her head other than to find and tell Jeff.

A lamp was lighted on the lower front gallery of the old Fleury house, and Dr. Hollingsworth was seated beside it in a wicker chair. He was smoking a cigar and reading.

'Alice, dear girl!' he said as she rushed up the steps and paused breathless before him. His professional training took a clinical look at her eyes, at the tremor in her fingers that held, as if with an ague, the edge of a piece of satin. 'You have had a shock.'

'Yes, Doctor — this.'

'It looks like — it's a doll's dress, isn't it?'

'It's the one Elsie was sewing on in the gazebo just before she disappeared.'

'Elsie? Oh, of course — the little Grunwald girl.'

'I must show it to Jeff.'

'But why?'

'There is a message stitched on it in Morse code. We had both learned the code together. It's Elsie's last message, Doctor.'

'Amazing!'

Alice took the gown from his fingers and said, 'I'll go right in, if you don't mind, and tell Jeff.'

'He isn't home.'

Delay was a blow.

'Do you know where he is?'

'No. Jeff has been taking long walks these nights. Alone. Trying to knock himself out physically so that he can get some sleep. Alice, sit down. Since you can't tell Jeff, tell me.'

This Alice did, from the birthday party down to the call from Mrs. Fleury and the motto and the stitches in Morse.

'What was your father's reaction? Is he getting in touch with the sheriff?'

'He knows nothing about it. It hit me so hard, Doctor, that I simply raced over here to tell Jeff. If I had met Papa on the way out I'd naturally have told him, but I didn't.'

'What did the message say, Alice?'

'I haven't decoded it yet because I'm waiting to do it with Jeff. I'm certain it will give us a clue to Elsie's kidnapping, and I know this sounds fantastic, but I honestly believe that Mrs. Fleury is right and that it will help Jeff, too. Do you think I'm being sentimentally impossible, Doctor?'

'Not that you feel that way, no. As I recall it, you were firmly convinced that Mrs. Fleury was a witch. I'd simply say that your subconscious was getting in a few old licks.'

'I'm almost ready to believe in her sorcery again, Doctor. Take her telephoning, the cracker bonbon, and the motto — she even spoke of a witch's broom — oh, it's not only Mrs. Fleury herself, it's the whole atmosphere of this place where she lived.'

'Witch's broom?'

'Yes. Witches'-broom is a growth that looks like a little broom. Of course you don't remember, but you caught some in the cuff of your trousers when you were looking over the grounds here with the real estate agent, and Jeff found it on the floor of your bedroom in the beach hotel.'

'Yes, now I do remember him asking me about it and I remember that when we moved in here he located the spot it came from. A clump of ferns. Serpent ferns, I think he called them.'

'Do you remember where they are?'

'I believe so, in a general way. They're back quite a distance in this tropical jungle. Why?'

'I want to go there. Could we go there,

Doctor? Now? While we're waiting for Jeff?'

'I suppose we could. But why?'

'I don't know why. This is crazy, but it's almost as if Mrs. Fleury were urging me to.'

Dr. Hollingsworth looked at Alice judicially, as if he were trying to determine a proper course of therapy for her evident emotional state.

'You are overstrung, Alice. The walk might be good for you at that.'

'Then you'll show me?'

'I'll get a flashlight,' Dr. Hollingsworth said.

★　★　★

Mr. Wickershield had been in the library, selecting a book for a quiet hour's reading, when he was conscious, as he thought, of a screen door slamming. Alice? Scarcely. Alice did not allow screen doors to slam. Still, that phone call from Mrs. Fleury had — just what had it done? Sort of knocked her for a loop, he decided.

Mr. Wickershield left the library and

170

rapped on Alice's door, then went inside. She wasn't there. The only light on was the desk lamp with its cone of brilliance from the metal shade. Inescapably his attention was drawn to the doll and to the flattened wrapper of the cracker bonbon. He went to the desk and sat down. Clearly, vividly, as though it were today, recognition came, and he recalled the whole grim episode of the birthday party, the kidnapping of Elsie, and that child of nine who had believed in the wondrous and was now his grown-up daughter Alice.

Something was missing. Of course — the doll dress that Elsie had been sewing and in which Alice had wrapped the cracker bonbon. Had she taken it with her when, judging from the screen-door slam, she had pelted from the house? To show Jeff? Most likely.

The end of the motto strip was exposed beneath the cracker bonbon wrapper, and he pulled it out. He read it. Thoughtfully he read it again.

Mr. Wickershield had served in Army Intelligence during the war, and his brain

171

was experienced in appraisal and deduction well beyond that of an untrained man. Alice had found some clue in the doll's dress to Elsie's disappearance and had rushed over to discuss it with Jeff — that line of deduction was almost obvious.

He then recalled the children's plunge into Morse code, so the connection between the motto and some probable stitching on the doll dress and the penciled letters on the paper wrapper suggested itself at once.

His experience with decoding in Intelligence had been superficial, but he saw immediately that this message (that must, he thought, have been stitched with such haste and yet such care, and under God knew what a pall of terror) was scarcely a code at all.

Comprehension iced his blood as he deciphered it and he started out at a brisk pace for the Grunwald home to pick up Hal.

★　★　★

The flashlight was powerful, one of those two-foot, heavy, cylindrical cases that could throw a beam an eighth of a mile, much farther than was needed for the job on hand.

'Well, there it is,' Dr. Hollingsworth said. 'The serpent ferns and the witches'-broom. Tell me, Alice, what really made you want to come here? I don't mind admitting that I am interested in extra-sensory perception, but in all reality I'm an out-and-out realist. Putting Mrs. Fleury's alleged witchery aside, why did you want to come?'

'Because there is something here.'

'What?'

'Doctor, I don't know. That it is connected with Elsie I do know, even though I don't know the reason.'

Alice parted the serpent ferns and took several hesitant steps within the large, lush clump.

'No need to be definite,' Dr. Hollingsworth said. 'Just tell me what you feel.'

'I feel a grave. I feel it is Elsie's, but I can't explain.'

Dr. Hollingsworth moved the light

shaft from the serpent ferns full upon Alice's face.

'The answer is simple, Alice,' he said. 'You are standing on it now.'

★   ★   ★

Both Mr. Wickershield and Hal had wasted no time. To reach the steps of the old Fleury house was but a matter of minutes. Hal knocked on the screen door, through which they could see a dimly lighted stretch of empty hall. They waited a moment, then went inside.

'Anybody home?' Hal shouted, his voice unnaturally loud under the pressure of their dangerous urgency.

A door at the end of the hallway opened and Jeff came out. 'Who's shouting?' he said. 'Oh — oh, hello. I've been working in my lab and I thought the house was coming down.'

'Where is the doctor?' Mr. Wickershield asked tensely.

'I left him reading on the gallery about an hour ago. I've been shut up in the lab since then. Why?'

'Where's Alice?'

'I've no idea. Why?'

'She ran over here to see you. Ten or fifteen minutes ago.'

'Then where is she? I never heard a thing in the lab until your shout. What's the matter? What's happened?'

Mr. Wickershield explained tersely while blood receded from Jeff's face in an ebbing tide.

'Where would he have taken her?' Mr. Wickershield asked.

'I — think I know,' Jeff said.

★ ★ ★

Pinned like a specimen bug in the harsh shaft of the flashlight, still having no knowledge of what Elsie's last message had meant but no longer needing that knowledge now that the implication in Dr. Hollingsworth's statement about the grave was so plain, Alice strained every muscle toward flight. But her control was gone. She stood like a statue among the serpent ferns, marbleized by shock and fright.

'You killed Elsie,' she said in someone else's voice.

'Yes.'

'But you had everything — money, position — Why?'

'I had no money. I had spent the small fortune I killed my wife for. I needed more.'

'Your wife — then it wasn't a hit-and-run?'

'No. It was arranged.'

'But Elsie — a little child — '

'I suggest you think of her rather in terms of fifty thousand dollars, a sum I have pyramided through legitimate business channels into a comfortable fortune. There was no need to continue with crime. Only Sidonia Grunwald's erratic prying around here offered any threat. Well, an appropriate opportunity presented itself and I took advantage of it.'

'You involved Jeff. You are making him pay. Don't you love him? If you don't, if you never have, why did you adopt him?'

'For a front.'

'Front?'

'Like the flower shops the Chicago

gangsters used to run. Gave them a legitimate surface of respectability. Jeff did that for me.'

'How?'

'As a son he gave me the desirable standing of being a family man, a good, kind father to a well-brought-up boy. A lone bachelor or a widower is always an object of speculative curiosity, whereas a father with a child is hardly ever suspected. Having reached my goal of financial security, however, Jeff became expendable.'

'You arranged it so that they would believe he had hit Mrs. Grunwald.'

'Of course. He stopped the car and passed out at the start of the driveway. Sidonia was going on with her act that night. I trailed her, as I usually had, heard the car, saw Jeff's drunken condition as he slumped over the wheel, and appreciated the perfect setup.' Dr. Hollingsworth added matter-of-factly, 'Before arranging her in the condition in which she was found, I hit her with this flashlight.'

★ ★ ★

Although the moon was at the full, its blue-white brightness rinsed but sparsely through the tropical overhead as Jeff led the way.

'Move quietly so as not to startle him,' Mr. Wickershield warned, the words thick from dread. 'There may still be time.'

Shortly Jeff stopped.

'They're over there,' he said. 'Step here and you can see the beam from his flashlight — there, through that break in the shrubs.'

Mr. Wickershield moved beside Jeff and saw it, saw it focused on Alice's rigid face.

Then saw it go out.

'Run for it!' he said.

It was Jeff who caught Dr. Hollingsworth's upraised arm before the torch could crash down again.

★　★　★

The following evening, feeling somewhat like Madame Récamier with her famous levees-a-la-chaise-longue, Alice lay on a bamboo counterpart in the company of her father, Jeff, and Bill Duggan, chief investigator for the sheriff's department. Hal was not with them. He was at Memorial with Sidonia, who had passed the crisis and was given by the doctors a more than excellent chance for complete recovery.

Alice herself was fairly over the effects from the blow of the flashlight that had landed glancingly on her head before Jeff had put an end to the murderous attack.

'Evidence?' Duggan was saying. 'We're glutted with it. The district attorney looks like a canary-stuffed cat. That ransom note, the one the Grimwalds got eleven years ago, was still on file. The B.C.I. boys knew back then that it was written on a blank leaf torn from a book. From some particular book among the hundreds of thousands of books within the area, so that got them no place. But now it does. Once the message stitched on the doll dress put the finger on him, Dr. Hollingsworth's library was inspected, and the leaf was found to have been torn from a book on forensic medicine — a reference work he would have hesitated to throw away, even if he hadn't felt so sure of himself. Even the printing on the note, although he tried to disguise it, has been identified by an expert graphologist as being his.'

'Did the witches'-broom help?' Alice asked. 'The specimen Jeff kept?'

'Definitely. It puts him at the grave.'

'Why do you suppose he picked that special spot?' Jeff asked.

'He told me. It's all down in his statement. He picked the Fleury grounds because, for one thing, they were handy. After a very bad attempt at trying to wheedle Elsie into going to a movie with him, and obviously frightening her enough by his manner and insistence into stitching her message for help, he killed her. Then he carried her from the gazebo, and the large clump of serpent ferns hid her nicely until he buried her in the center of them that night. Naturally he could move about freely. There was no earthly reason why any suspicion would point to him.'

'Wouldn't the Everglades have been safer?' Mr. Wickershield asked. 'Some far-off place?'

'He said he had thought of that, then he thought that even if the body ever were discovered under the ferns Mrs. Fleury herself would provide an excellent suspect, what with her somewhat odd habits. Of course he didn't know then that she had a perfect alibi. Nobody knew until a couple of days later when we turned up the fact that she was in the beauty shop.'

'I can see why he bought the place as soon as it was put up for sale,' Mr. Wickershield said. 'He wouldn't want other tenants to have it. Their possible ideas on altering the landscaping could conceivably have uncovered the grave. I can even see how he might have got a perverted kick out of it, although Sidonia's prowlings must have kept him somewhat on edge.'

'No, for a while they kind of amused him, but the night he fixed up the drunk-driving deal on Jeff was different. You see, he had been tailing her as usual, and she did something that night she had never done before. Signed her own death warrant, you might say.'

'What was it?'

'She went into the utility room by the garage and came out with a shovel.'

Much later at night Duggan got home

and told his wife all about it.

'Like a fairy tale,' he said. 'Only a damn grim one. Take that coded message, and the uncanny way the motto pointed toward the sewing on the doll dress. Here — here's a copy. Mr. Wickershield spotted it right off as simple contraction.'

Mrs. Duggan looked at the slip of paper.

DRHOLCRZYHLPM
DR HOL CRZY HLP M
DOCTOR HOLLINGSWORTH CRAZY
HELP ME

'And the motto?' she asked.
'A stitch in time saves nine.'

Agree — Or Die

The Waldemar estate lazed in semi-tropical splendor the year round. Until, that is, the night of December 10, when Herbert Waldemar, blasted by gunfire, was found in one of its beach cabanas, dead. The case — so pat, so simple on its surface — hid perhaps the most provocative question since Frank R. Stockton posed his famous one concerning the lady or the tiger.

When we first knew the Waldemar family, Herbert had been in the process of marrying his fourth wife, and Ilya (my only one) had said with her usual passionate interest in the lives of others, 'I don't understand it. It's so completely off-beat.'

'Why shouldn't it be? If he wants it that way?'

'Because it breaks the pattern. Men who marry a lot always stick to the same last. If I died, Fred, you would settle on my duplicate.'

'Possibly, but how about the proverbial exception?'

'Not in this instance. The shift is too extreme. His other three were flaming creatures just one bikini this side of a strip tease, whereas Anne Borney — Well!'

There was a good deal, as it usually turns out, in what Ilya said. Anne Borney was Boston Back Bay and about as flaming as a thoughtful candle in a homestead window. Not that she was negative or in any sense lacking in personality; rather, you thought of her as the well-mannered surface of a glassy and unarresting tarn that filmed sleeping depths. My own wonderment lay not so much in why Waldemar was marrying Anne Borney as in why she was marrying him.

'Money,' Ilya said, putting me straight on it. 'And then, he's not entirely impossible, in spite of his steam-roller technique.' This was true because Waldemar, as a whole, was acceptably sleek, while escaping the oiliness of the glad-hand type of some hotel men. It was the minor facets that jarred, a feeling of reserved brutality, of a callousness that was thoroughly ruthless in its nature.

'Just the same, Ilya, a Boston Borney and a steam roller do not mix. I don't care how much cash is involved.'

'She had no choice.'

It is both ridiculous and a waste of time ever to question the accuracy of Ilya's information about anybody who has ruffled her curiosity. Almost without exception she will be suffocatingly right.

'What choice?'

'She couldn't take it any longer. Living on tactful handouts from her friends.'

It made sense, in spite of the natural reaction of questioning why Anne Borney didn't get herself a job, because at once you saw that she couldn't get a job. Her age was against her, as were her delicately horselike patrician looks and her entire background of well-bred but, in a business sense, useless Borney womanhood. Obviously it was a tossup between being a society charity case or taking a handful of sleeping pills, and charity in time wears thin, both for the donor and the donee.

'Had she no money at all? No solvent

relatives to turn to?'

'She has one brother, ten years younger, and what money she did have she wasted on him.'

'A charming bum?'

'A charming crook. Not that Peter Borney was ever indicted, but he did have connections.'

'Underworld?'

'Racketeering of some nature. He has the build of a chiseled ox and turned to bodyguarding one of the FBI's most desirable — in the sense of being wanted — men. I don't know who.'

'Why not?'

'Oh, really, Fred!'

'Is he still doing it? Usually such jobs pay well, so I don't see why Anne had to give him her pennies.'

'His boss died, by request, two years ago, and Peter has been living a model, if dependent, life since then.'

'Where is he now?'

'He is here for the wedding, of course.'

'Here' is Florida. The town of Halcyon, to be exact, on the east coast, to the north of Miami, where we bought a home after

I had retired and turned the operation of my private-investigation agency over to our son Frank. Frank is running it now from the main office in New York, commuting daily from his home in Scarsdale.

As for the Herbert Waldemar estate, it is ten times the size of our own, which is nothing remarkable when you consider that our incomes are equally disproportionate, Waldemar's being a golden flood from a chain of luxury motels located in key resort spots all over the country. His Halcyon operation is on the beach and caters to wealthy jewelers from Cleveland, ardent race-track connoisseurs, elegant divorcees, and a mélange of properly heeled sun chasers.

The wedding took place in the Waldemar patio on the afternoon of November 4. It was agreeably stereotyped in a champagne-and-caviar fashion, and the only moment of unusual interest occurred when I looked about for Ilya with the thought of breaking for home.

A casual search led through the estate's tropical garden and brought me face to face, in a secluded frangipani-scented corner, with the bride's scamp brother

Peter and a girl whom I recognized as being Waldemar's only child, Lace, the daughter of his first marriage. They were in what is referred to now, I understand, as a smooch. The term is vulgarly unjust because I caught a look in their eyes, when they came up for air, and in it lay love if ever one saw it.

I did my best to pass by in the manner of an elderly, if well preserved, blind bat, but Lace disengaged herself from the muscular arms of the chiseled ox and said in a voice that held a hint of worry and a premonition of heartbreak, 'We'd rather you didn't mention this, Mr. Brandt.'

'Of course I won't, Miss Waldemar.'

'To anybody.'

'Not even to Ilya.'

'You're very kind.'

There was an awkward second of parting, then they went off one way and I continued the hunt in another, finding Ilya by the swimming pool, tossing caviar canapés to an immersed male guest, who presumably was imitating a trained seal. Then we went home.

It stood to reason that any promised

silence concerning the Peter-Lace entanglement could not prevent the odds from hitting a hundred to one against Ilya scenting it out, and the odds were absolutely right.

'At first I took it for another off-beat note,' she said to me during breakfast several mornings later, 'but it's quite understandable, really.'

'Splendid.'

'You needn't upstage me, Fred. You've had your mind on it yourself.'

'I have?'

'You have. On the surface, Herbert's paternal opposition does seem contradictory. I mean, if Herbert accepted Anne Borney plus her tinged brother, why gag at Lace falling in love with him? Especially when you consider Herbert. No one would cast him as the puritanical type.'

'Scarcely.'

'But after a few odd bits of information,' Ilya went on, 'I realized that Herbert not only would oppose such a marriage but definitely had to arrange for a complete soft-pedaling of Peter and his ex-gangster milieu. I shouldn't wonder if Herbert made him a remittance man. Somewhere in Mexico or Asia.'

'Anne would never stand for it.'

'You'd be surprised at what Anne will have to stand for — Oh, I suppose I do overdo this being omniscient stuff, but can't you see?'

'Not having your innumerable sources of information, no.'

'It's because of a new motel Herbert is planning for Bar Harbor. Not like his other gaudy places. This one is to be Plaza, St. Regis, Ritz, in the most conservatively proper sense of the word. It's for Lace's sake, primarily. She's of marriageable age.'

'Light dimly dawns.'

'Of course it does. Of course it's why he married Anne. His other three were snap happenstances for their body content or what have you, but this marriage was calculatingly planned. A Boston Borney will be an impeccable magnet for an old-guard clientele, and the place itself a suitable fishing bowl for Lace.'

'With brother Peter presenting the only soup stain on the joint's escutcheon.'

'Exactly. It will be interesting to see just what sort of spot remover Herbert selects.'

'There is a sort of slow-fuse feeling about all this.'

'I rather wondered when you'd get around to that.' Then Ilya added absently as she left the table to start out for her morning round of pitiable golf, 'Herbert is thinking of calling the new motel The Borney Arms.'

★　★　★

It was several weeks later — on the eve of the fatal December 10, to pin-point it — when Anne Borney cornered me on the veranda of the Dolphin Club during a standard Saturday-night scrimmage. Possibly it was the moonlight that made her look so pale and somewhat like an unauthorized ghost out of *Hamlet*. She came directly to the point.

'I should like your help, Mr. Brandt. I am worried about Herbert.'

'In what way, Mrs. Waldemar?'

'Naturally you are familiar with the past fight between the Hotel Owners

Association and the organizers who were sent down to force an acceptance of the Hotel Employees Union.'

'Yes.'

'Also, that an agreement has been reached and signed. As I understand it from Herbert, it is not compulsory and some of the operators are still holding out. Herbert is one of them. Herbert is possibly the most virulently antagonistic of them all.'

'Are you implying threats?'

'Yes.'

'Surely not directly? The union people would never be so stupid.'

'Naturally not. It is being done obliquely through a so-called 'protective' association. It has been pointed out to Herbert that unless he unionizes, or whatever the proper term is, he is laying himself open to reprisals. The association has offered to protect him from those reprisals. At a price.'

'It's a familiar pattern, Mrs. Waldemar. I think your husband can discount entirely that the union is in any way connected with such a setup. You'll find it's an independent racket — some of the would-be bright boys cashing in on the local situation.'

'Does it matter who they are? So far as Herbert's safety is concerned?'

'His personal safety? Surely that's going pretty far. Perhaps there'll be some sabotage in the linen, utilities put out of commission by imported goons — but not murder.'

Anne Borney pressed for a moment against the veranda railing, her face moon-white toward the horizon of the metallic silvered sea.

'Why not? Why not murder, Mr. Brandt, as an example to the other owners who are holding out?'

'You keep harping on the thought almost as though your husband had received a definite threat.'

'He has. He threw the association man out on his ear. That was two days ago, and yesterday morning there was that message written in the hard sand left by ebb tide.'

'On your beach?'

'Yes. The message read: *Waldemar, agree — or die.* No more. Just the four words. Herbert said it struck him as laughable. He stamped them out.'

The message was, of course, not only rankly melodramatic but downright corny. It reeked of the amateur, and I said so, adding that the very location of the message was absurd. A billboard could scarcely have been more public or spectacular.

'Not really, Mr. Brandt. Our beach boy doesn't go on duty until eight, and Herbert always takes a morning plunge at seven. The beach is quite private.'

'Did Mr. Waldemar broadcast the discovery?'

'Only to us at breakfast. He made some weighty jokes about it.'

'Lace and Peter were with you?'

'Yes. It was a send-off meal in a way. Peter caught a plane shortly afterward for the Bahamas. Herbert is sending him on a tour of the islands and later to South America to look up potential motel sites. Herbert's motto would seem to be: Expansion.'

(How right, as per schedule, Ilya had been! Remittance stuff in acceptable camouflage.)

'You said I might help you, Mrs. Waldemar. How?'

'I should like to arrange through your agency for a guard. I understand your son now runs it, but perhaps you would take it up with him for me?'

'I should be glad to, but would Mr. Waldemar agree?'

'Frankly, no. I should like him to be protected without his knowledge. Can it be done?'

'It would be difficult, but possible. I'll call Frank in the morning.'

But Waldemar was dead by morning.

There were four gunshot wounds in various parts of Waldemar's anatomy, and the shots had been fired from a sufficient distance so that the bullets had remained in the body. Upon being extracted, they proved to have come from four guns of different calibers — a .38 S & W revolver, a .32 Colt automatic pistol, a .30 Luger, and a .455-caliber bullet tentatively identified as having been shot from a British Webley-Fosbery semi-automatic. Time of death: roughly between 2 and 3 a.m.

These technical details were given us by Bill Duggan, who is the chief criminal investigator for our sheriff's department.

We are good friends, and he occasionally drops in on Ilya and me for a bull session about criminals who (either because of his personal or my agency's more collective smartnesses) had bit the dust.

Duggan's fondness for clichés amounts almost to a vice, and he announced flatly, 'This case is open and shut.'

'So it would seem,' I agreed, while Ilya remained commentless and continued with a lilac cashmere stole she was knitting for herself for Christmas.

Succinctly, the official version was that four hoods, imported by the 'protective' association for general sabotage and terrorization, had done the job. They were already in custody and being held for the grand jury on suspicion of Murder One. As each relied on the other three for an alibi, said alibis canceled each other out, amounting to zero. The four murder guns undoubtedly were silted at the bottom of the Atlantic Ocean.

A note signed Floss had been found among other personal papers on the desk in Waldemar's room when it had been gone through by the boys. The note had arranged for a 2 a.m. rendezvous at the scene of the crime, the beach cabana, and Floss had been identified as Miss Bubble Girl of 1957 in one of Miami's more lurid traps. It was current gossip among her professional set that she was hopeful of becoming, at some future convenient date, Mrs. Waldemar Number Five.

Floss tigerishly denied having written the note, and a check of her handwriting proved the point. It was officially accepted, however, that she knew about it, inasmuch as she was un-platonically involved with one of the four apprehended hoods, and a check of his handwriting proved the note to have been written by him.

This he admitted, and further admitted (after a session of judiciously expert treatment only remotely connected with a Swedish massage) that he and his three confreres had gone to the cabana to beat Waldemar up, but the four of them screamed their heads off that Waldemar was already dead when they got there. Both the police and the sheriff's department thought this very amusing.

'The whole thing is in the bag,' Duggan

said contentedly.

'They used the note to put him on the spot. Furthermore, even if the trial should slip up here, which it won't, the bums are wanted for the death of the little Bixby boy in St. Louis and for the shotgun blasting of the girl bank teller in Denver. Come hell or high water, those buzzards are due to fry. You can take your pick of for what.'

Matters turned out quite along the line that Duggan had forecast. The grand jury returned a true bill, and the four were indicted for murder in the first degree. (Floss was exonerated as having been an unknowing dupe in regard to the murderous purpose of the assignation note, and returned to her bubbles.) Two months later, in March, the gunmen were brought to trial, found guilty, and sentenced to the chair during the week of June 10–17. Appeals were denied, and on June 13 they were electrocuted.

On what might be called the social side of this period, affairs also progressed. Lace inherited her father's large fortune, with Anne getting her widow's third — a fortune in itself — while Peter returned promptly from his motel site-viewing tour and married Lace in a very quiet and unpublicized wedding.

It was pleasant to consider how just Fate was with its comeuppances. There seemed little question but that Waldemar had been a viciously ruthless and selfish man in his private life. Even though I knew nothing about them personally, with the exception of Anne, his three former wives had been flesh and blood, with all the feelings that women have and all their capacities for being hurt. Especially this must have been true about the first one, Lace's mother, for surely Lace was a reflection of her and not of Waldemar. Yet he had used these women more as bought-and-paid-for mistresses than as wives and, becoming tired of them, had callously, brutally (according to the records) kicked them out. Now he was dead.

And the four hoods found guilty of killing him were dead too. If any men deserved execution, they did. There was no question of their guilt in the Bixby boy case in St. Louis, which Duggan had referred to, nor in the wanton slaying of the girl bank teller in Denver.

Nor did there seem any reasonable question regarding their shooting of Waldemar, even though the state's case had been purely circumstantial and all four had maintained their innocence to the end. As Duggan had said, 'No matter for what,' they had got what they deserved.

Yes, everybody was satisfied.

Except Ilya.

'Tell me, Fred,' she said during supper on the evening after the execution, 'how do you feel about Weismann's theory on genes and on heredity in general?'

'I feel nothing, Ilya. I don't even know what his theory is.'

'It's about passing character traits on from parent to child during successive generations — traits like horse stealing or homicidal mania. Weismann was a nineteenth-century contemporary of Mendel and Darwin, and his contention is that inheritance consists in determinants which cause character traits to appear — rather, to reappear — *under the right conditions*. If the conditions aren't right, the traits still keep passing on from parent to child but they stay dormant. Until.'

'I take it you mean that if Captain Kidd or Jack the Ripper were my ancestors, their bloodletting proclivities might have lain dormant in my father, grandfather, and et cetera, only to come suddenly to life again in me if the conditions were right?'

'Precisely.'

'Well, so what? Why bring the subject up?'

'Because it explains the murder of Herbert. Those four men never killed him, of course.'

I'll admit I felt shaken. In the several homicide cases our agency had handled (our work deals largely with defalcations in banks and corporations), Ilya's perception and judgment had been infallible. And they had not been based upon that kicked around commodity known as woman's intuition. If she was right in the Waldemar instance, then who *had* killed him? Well, Peter stuck out like a sore thumb as a prime suspect.

'I suppose, Ilya, in your sibylline

fashion you are getting around to the revelation that Peter collected four hoods from his gangster-association days and arranged the deal while he alibied himself in the Bahamas?'

'I am not. Peter had nothing to do with it.'

'Well, Lace certainly didn't, nor Anne.'

'Not Lace.'

'Anne?'

'Who else?'

Like a fool, I laughed. Heartily. A mental picture of the gently bred and nurtured Anne Borney hiring four gunmen, even if she would remotely know how to get in touch with four paid killers, was too much. I said so.

'What is more,' I added, 'why should she? She'd made a bargain with Waldemar when she married him and she's the type of woman who would keep it.'

'Granted. Provided the other person to the bargain kept his side of it. You know perfectly well that, as soon as Herbert got all he wanted from her, Anne would have been out on her ear again. With that Floss or some other bubble-dancing expert sliding into her place.'

'That is still no reason for murder — definitely not for a woman of Anne's background and character.'

Ilya sighed patiently.

'I've been in touch during the past few months with Marion Dorchester in Boston,' she said. (I remembered Miss Dorchester vaguely as being one of Ilya's elderly spinster friends.) 'Marion is an officer in one of the genealogical societies of Massachusetts and I asked her to trace the Borney line back.'

'Why?'

'Because the same doubts puzzled me that are now puzzling you. Marion didn't finish her research — that sort of digging takes ages — until this morning and she called me up. The electrocution was an accomplished fact by then, of course. It's pretty amazing what Marion unearthed, Fred.'

'A celebrated murder in the family tree?'

'No. Marion traced the line back into the fifteenth century, when the Borney name was spelled Bonny. Back to the days of pirates. Two of whom were women. You'll find them listed in the Encyclopedia Britannica. A Mary Read was one of them. The other was named Anne Bonny.'

'Anne Borney — '

'Think of her as Anne Bonny. Think of Herbert Waldemar as the bullion-laden prize frigate that would get her and Peter out of all their difficulties. *Think*, Fred.'

'I am thinking. I'm thinking of the mechanics of Waldemar's murder. Regardless of her inherited piratical potentialities, I'm thinking of the difficulty — the impossibility, really — of a woman like Anne Borney getting in touch with and hiring four professional killers.'

'She didn't. She accomplished what amounts to the perfect crime. The case is closed and no evidence exists to open it up again. Anne easily could have found that note from Floss making the assignation in the cabana. The hoods undoubtedly kept the rendezvous and did find Herbert dead. Anne simply managed to get there first. She had plenty of time between finding the note and two o'clock in the morning to make arrangements.'

'Are you crazy, Ilya? Time to shop around and pick up four killers — as if she were shopping for a hat?'

'I am not crazy, Fred, and she didn't pick up four killers. I told you this was the perfect crime. It was accepted by the police exactly for what it was intended — a mobster killing. Anne handled it entirely by herself. Guns can be bought a dime a dozen here in Florida, and no questions asked. Anne simply bought four pistols of different calibers and put one shot from each into Herbert.'

'Not Anne — '

'Anne Borney, no. But the no-longer-dormant determinants and piratical traits of Anne Bonny, yes. Blood, Fred, will tell.'

The question raised was staggering.

Had blood told?

Or had it not?

What do you think? The lady — or the pirate?